# DEAD
# BIG DAWG

# DEAD
# BIG DAWG

## A Loon Lake Mystery

# VICTORIA HOUSTON

**G**

**Gallery Books**

New York   London   Toronto   Sydney   New Delhi

# G

Gallery Books
An Imprint of Simon & Schuster, Inc.
1230 Avenue of the Americas
New York, NY 10020

First Gallery Books trade paperback edition June 2019

GALLERY BOOKS and colophon are registered trademarks of Simon & Schuster, Inc.

For information about special discounts for bulk purchases, please contact Simon & Schuster Special Sales at 1-866-506-1949 or business@simonandschuster.com.

The Simon & Schuster Speakers Bureau can bring authors to your live event. For more information or to book an event, contact the Simon & Schuster Speakers Bureau at 1-866-248-3049 or visit our website at www.simonspeakers.com.

Interior design by Davina Mock-Maniscalco

Manufactured in the United States of America

10   9   8   7   6   5   4   3   2

Library of Congress Cataloging-in-Publication Data
Names: Houston, Victoria, 1945– author.
Title: Dead big dawg / Victoria Houston.
Description: First Gallery Books trade paperback edition. | New York : Gallery Books, 2019. | Series: A Loon Lake mystery ; 19
Identifiers: LCCN 2018060608 (print) | LCCN 2019000053 (ebook) | ISBN 9781440598852 (ebook) | ISBN 9781440598838 (trade paperback : alk. paper)
Subjects: | BISAC: FICTION / Mystery & Detective / Women Sleuths. | FICTION / Mystery & Detective / General. | GSAFD: Mystery fiction.
Classification: LCC PS3608.O88 (ebook) | LCC PS3608.O88 D427 2019 (print) | DDC 813/.6—dc23
LC record available at https://lccn.loc.gov/2018060608

ISBN 978-1-4405-9883-8
ISBN 978-1-4405-9885-2 (ebook)

*For Jason and Vesper*

*No one forgets the truth.*
*They just get better at lying.*
Richard Yates, *Revolutionary Road*


*A perfect cast is a thing of beauty.*
*It is like a note of music extended and held.*
Joan Wulff, *Joan Wulff's Fly Casting Techniques*

# CHAPTER ONE

Staring into the eyes of the great horned owl, the old woman died happy.

They had been meeting like this for months: in the dark, in secrecy. Watching one another, sometimes watching the creatures moving through the towering pines surrounding them . . . just . . . watching.

The owl had seen her head move as the bullet slammed into her brain. Death was painless, even as the brilliance of her mind was extinguished.

When the old woman had lain still too long, when her eyes no longer met his, the owl sent the alert. Within seconds the forest surrounding Loon Lake erupted with alarms as owls woke their feathered cousins to pass along the warning.

---

Eight-year-old Cody Amundson, fishing in the dark off his grandfather's dock, paused before casting his lure. The explosion of birdcalls caught him by surprise. Turning toward shore, he was scanning the pine boughs over his head when a scream pierced the air. Throwing his spinning rod into the rowboat moored alongside the dock, Cody ran up the stone stairway leading to his grandfather's house. He banged through the porch door and right into the arms of Dr. Paul Osborne.

"Shhhh. Settle down, Cody. It's okay," said Osborne, grasping the trembling boy firmly by the shoulders. "Just a screech owl."

"Are you sure, Gramps? That sounds like a real person. Maybe we should call Chief Ferris?"

During the same five minutes since the birds had started calling, Ray Pradt had paused to look up from where he was dousing a campfire he had built in hopes of charming his date.

"My God, Ray, what is that racket?" asked the young woman, looking up as she opened the screen door to the trailer. A bat swooped and she nearly dropped the bowl of chips and guacamole she was carrying back to the kitchen.

Before Ray could answer, a harsh cry echoed through the trees.

"What on earth? Who the hell was *that*?" The girl was happy to close the door behind her. "Boy, is this a fun place."

Paraphrasing his neighbor's words to his grandson, Ray assured Paula that a serial killer was not lurking in the dark. "That's an owl, not a human," said Ray, following her into his trailer as the embers died in the fire pit behind him. "And don't you worry—I know how to keep you safe. . . ."

"Yeah, right." The girl grinned as she let him wrap his arms around her.

---

Next door, once Cody nodded that he believed his grandfather, Osborne walked the boy back down to the dock to retrieve his fishing rod. "Okay, son? Not afraid anymore?" Osborne kept a reassuring hand on the boy's shoulder. "We don't want your new rod to end up in the lake, so let's put it away in my fish hut where it'll be safe."

Cody relaxed as he stepped into the rowboat to retrieve his rod. Any time spent in Grandpa's fish hut was okay with him.

———————

Early the next morning before Cody was up, Osborne was enjoying his coffee on the screened-in porch when Ray gave a quick knock on the porch door before walking in, coffee mug in hand. "Morning, Doc. Did you hear that scream last night?"

"Scared the living daylights out of Cody."

"One more little bunny who won't need a hat," said Ray as he filled his mug from the pot Osborne kept plugged in on the porch.

"That wasn't a rabbit, that was a screech owl."

"Oh . . . Hmm, wonder what the birds saw. They were pretty excited. . . ."

The men sipped their coffee: Osborne on his porch swing, Ray in his favorite chair, and the sun throwing shadows on the dock as early summer infused the lake world with life.

# CHAPTER TWO

"H-e-e-e-y, Cody, Becky . . . Breakfast is ready. Hurry, hurry, hurry before it gets cold."

Lewellyn Ferris hoped her voice would carry over the broad expanse of grass that swept down to the water's edge where the dock was still submerged thanks to late-spring rains. She had warned the kids not to play down there, but she knew kids. "Hey, you two," she called again, "pancakes are ready. Better hurry up—"

She turned back toward the screen door leading into the tiny red frame house she lovingly referred to as "my farm," though no one had raised a calf on the ancient dairy farm in over fifty years. "I beg your pardon, my place is *absolutely* a farm," she would counter when Osborne teased her about the old place.

"I have a wonderful organic garden, an asparagus patch that's over a hundred years old, and acres of milkweed for raising monarch butterflies. So what if I don't have cows or goats—I still *farm*."

Smiling at the determination in her voice, Osborne would refuse to concede: "Yeah, well you're also the Loon Lake chief of police and you love to spend time in the trout stream—so when exactly is it that you find time to farm?"

It was an argument neither of them ever won.

———————————

Today, blessed with a rare long weekend off from official duties and commandeered to host her granddaughter while her daughter attended a friend's wedding over in the cities, she had invited Osborne and his grandson, Cody, for breakfast. Minutes earlier, with the first round of pancakes ready to come off the grill, she'd made another suggestion: "So, Doc, why don't you leave Cody here for the day? He can keep Becky company while I plant my tomatoes."

"While you *farm*?" Osborne had grinned. With a fake grimace, Lew slapped three pancakes on his plate, then kissed the top of his head.

The two kids were the same age and had played together many times before, as their respective grandparents had been close friends now for over three years. ("My mom says they're sweethearts," Lew had heard Becky explain to Cody during one of their play dates).

Waiting to hear the screen door open, Lew watched Osborne prepare his plate of buckwheat pancakes. After buttering each and stacking them one atop the other, he picked up the jug of maple syrup and poured . . . and poured and . . . "Omygod, Doc. That is one hell of a lot of syrup—especially for a dentist. . . ."

"*Retired* dentist," said Osborne, adopting a serious tone. "Don't remind me. I love pancakes." Just as he was savoring his first forkful, Lew disappeared out the door to call the kids again.

A minute later she was back in the sunny kitchen, her eyes serious. "No sign of the little stinkers and I told them to stay close by. Now what kind of trouble can those two get into on a gorgeous day like this? Doc, I'm going to check on them. Something doesn't feel right."

With a sigh, Osborne slipped his plate into the warm oven and followed her out the door.

No sign of two children anywhere along the shoreline of the small lake bordering Lew's property; a quick look inside the ancient barn where a previous owner had once raised dairy cows revealed only a nest of newborn rabbits; and a sprint down the driveway to the main road ended with no one in sight.

"Okay," said Lew, thinking, "the neighbors across the hill. . . ." She pointed west. "They have a new puppy, and I'll bet you anything Becky took Cody over to play with the little guy. That *has* to be where they are." Osborne could hear the worry in her voice, and he didn't blame her.

As they ran along a narrow path leading through shin-high grass, Osborne had to admire Lew's conditioning. Though she was in her early fifties with a sturdy, not slender, build—she ran like an athlete. He, meanwhile, was breathing hard, hoping they might reach the neighbors' before he had a heart attack.

The path ran along a low wooden fence, which they clambered over; then they pushed their way through a tangle of balsam saplings to arrive in view of the neighbors' driveway. Thank the Lord, thought Osborne.

Even though she could hear Doc breathing hard, Lew didn't slow down. She kept running: past the modest frame structure where the family lived and around to the back, where an old barn had been converted to house a sawmill operation. Three cars were parked in front of the building.

With a swift intake of breath, Lew recognized the vehicles: official cars. Official, she knew, from the government license plates and the outline of emergency lights visible through the rear windows. FBI? State investigators? Was someone hurt?

Refusing to think past the moment, she dashed forward, Osborne right behind her. Two small figures emerged from between two of the cars and ran toward them. "Oh, Grandpa, it's so exciting!" shouted Cody, waving his arms and hopping up and down. "Becky and I saw everything—" Before he could finish, a man walked up behind the two children.

"Chief Ferris?" asked the man, sounding as stupefied at the sight of her as she was at the sight of him. She was looking directly at the director of the FBI's statewide cybersecurity team whom she'd met at a conference in Green Bay just one month earlier.

# CHAPTER THREE

**D**ick French? What are you doing here? What did these kids do? That one's my granddaughter—"

Lew threw her questions at the last person she expected to see in Loon Lake, much less her neighbors' yard. As she strode quickly toward French, she spotted her neighbors, Vern and Marge Neustrom, watching from where they were standing, holding their barn doors open so two other men could carry large cardboard boxes into the building.

"Boy, am I surprised to see you out here in the boonies, Chief Ferris," said French. "And don't worry—the kids are fine. These two youngsters came running up right as we pulled in and did just what we asked. Didn't you." He patted Cody on the head. "They took orders like professionals and stayed out of our way."

He turned away from Cody. "Excuse me, sir." French took a step toward Osborne, who had run up to stand beside Lew. "If Chief Ferris won't introduce us, let me—"

"Oh, I am so sorry," said Lew. "Dick, this is my good friend Dr. Paul Osborne. We were just about to have pancakes with our grandkids—his and mine, whom you just met." She pointed at Cody and Becky. "Doc," she said, turning to Osborne, "I'd like you to meet Dick French. I know Dick from his work running the FBI's cybersecurity team out of Green Bay."

"Haven't I heard or seen your name somewhere, Dr. Osborne?" asked French.

"You may," said Lew before Osborne could open his mouth. "Doc is a retired dentist with expertise in dental forensics so both myself and the Wausau Crime Lab lean on him when we need an expert on odontology."

"Hold on now," said Osborne. "Chief Ferris is overstating my credentials, I'm afraid. Let's just say I know whom to ask when they need an expert analysis," said Osborne, anxious for his skills not to be oversold to the FBI.

"Well, Dr. Osborne, Chief Ferris, the good news is you can go back to your pancakes," said French. "We're finished here for the moment—"

"For the moment? What does that mean exactly?" asked Lew.

"You may find this hard to believe but the Neustroms' old PC, the computer they keep here in the barn to use for billing customers of their sawmill operation, has been taken over by hackers out of Russia."

"You must be kidding—Russian hackers in the heart of the northwoods?" Lew couldn't keep the astonishment out of her voice. She resisted the urge to laugh.

"Yep, a young guy on our team flagged suspicious activity two days ago when someone tried to breach the security of one of the larger health insurers. We traced the activity back to this location." Lew started to open her mouth, but he put up a hand to stop her. "Hold on—the Neustroms have nothing to do with this, Chief. The hackers took over their computer and have been using it to stage attacks on a number of sites."

"So are you shutting it down? Destroying the hard drive and—"

"None of the above. Certainly not until we know exactly who the hackers are. In the meantime, we've already started to monitor their activity remotely. Two of my team members will be here over the weekend. They will keep the garage under surveillance until the chief security officer with a firm that tracks digital attacks gets here Monday.

"Get to know her, Chief. Her name is Diane Armeo, and she was formerly with the National Security Agency (NSA). She cofounded the cybersecurity company that'll be watching this." He grinned. "She's a damn good hacker herself in case you want lessons. I hope you'll make her welcome. I'll give her your name and let her know you live nearby."

"Of course," said Lew. "Let me give you my personal cell number, too. And what about the Neustroms? Do they need anything?"

"I don't think so. They've been very cooperative. We are setting them up with a new computer for their bookkeeping and trying to stay out of the way of their business. If you see anything they might need or have a problem with, please let me know."

"They must be surprised as hell," said Osborne. "I sure am."

"We all are," said French. "But we're excited, too. This is one of only ten sites like this that we've been able to locate in the country."

"And who would ever expect to find this in northern Wisconsin?" Osborne's question was rhetorical.

"Precisely. On the other hand, that may be no accident."

---

Romping through the high grass, Cody and Becky led their grandparents back to the promised pancakes. "Well, that's one way to start the weekend," said Osborne, eyebrows raised as he walked alongside Lew after deciding he'd done enough running for the day.

"I plan to be very happy planting tomatoes," said Lew. "And don't forget that Suzanne is treating us to fish fry tonight."

"Oh no, I forgot all about your daughter's generous offer," said Osborne, wincing. "I had a call from Mallory last night saying she was driving up from Chicago to spend the weekend. She isn't coming alone, either, as there seems to be a new boyfriend."

"Bring 'em along," said Lew with a wave of her hand. "I'd like to meet him. And Suzanne was leaning on me to include Ray, too." She paused. "Or would that be a problem? I know that he and Mallory were once—"

"A long time ago," said Osborne. "But doesn't Suzanne know better? Ray is entertaining but . . ." He didn't need to finish. Lew was well informed on Ray and women.

"She's a big girl," said Lew, "with two children and an accounting business to run. If she chooses to complicate her life that's her problem. Meantime, I'll tell her to forget buying dinner. We'll go Dutch. Be fun to see everyone."

"And we'll have the kids along, too. Right?"

"Oh yeah—including Ray." Lew rolled her eyes.

"Like you said, Lew, should be an entertaining evening," said Osborne.

"Say, Doc, did you leave any syrup?" Lew asked as they walked into the kitchen where the kids were already seated at the table.

"Oh, golly, not sure." Osborne grinned.

# CHAPTER FOUR

"Hey, Cody, what's the deal—you run away from home? Move in with Grandpa?" Sliding into the chair beside her father, Osborne's oldest daughter reached over to tickle her nephew.

"No, Aunt Mallory," said Cody, giggling as he squirmed. "Mom and Dad are at Mason's soccer tournament so I get to stay at Grandpa's." A sudden thought wiped the smile from his face: "But, um, I'm sleeping in your room. Do you want it back?" Worry clouded his eyes.

"Heavens, no," said Mallory, raising her voice over the din of voices in the Loon Lake Pub, "thank you, Cody, but this is one weekend when I need my privacy." She grinned as she spoke, adding, "Josh and I'll be staying at the Crescent Lake Motor Lodge. You have to come swim with us—they have a beautiful sandy beach. Or you and Grandpa can take Josh fishing."

"And exactly who *is* Josh?" asked Osborne, resting an arm across his daughter's shoulders. "And where is he? I thought he was driving up with you."

While Osborne was quizzing Mallory, Lew walked up with Suzanne and Becky. The three of them pulled out chairs and sat down, leaving only two empty at the large round table.

After pausing to say hello and introduce herself to Becky, Mallory glanced over at her father. "To answer your question, Dad, my friend's name is Josh Garner, and we've been dating for two months. Right now he's over at Ralph's Sporting Goods buying a fishing license. He should be here any minute."

As she was talking, a man wearing a light blue button-down shirt, its sleeves rolled up, and a pair of well-creased khakis walked up behind her, gave her shoulders a quick squeeze, and looked around at everyone seated at the table.

"A pleasure to meet you, Dr. Osborne, and you must be Chief Ferris," said Josh, extending a hand to each before being introduced to Suzanne and the kids. As he pulled out one of the two remaining empty chairs, Josh gave a quick glance at the hubbub behind him. "Wow—this place is busy. Is it always this crowded?"

---

Though the question was directed to him, Osborne was speechless at the sight of Mallory's new friend. Later he would confess to Lew that he had been taken aback at Josh's apparent youth, so much so that at first he hadn't known what to say.

"Lewellyn, the guy has to be fresh out of college. And, good grief, Mallory is over thirty years old, divorced and vice president of a large public relations firm. What is she thinking? What is *he* thinking?"

"Mind your own business, Doc," Lew had said.

---

Tackling Osborne's befuddled silence, Lew spoke up, saying, "Friday night fish fry, Josh—an iconic event here in the northwoods where beer-battered fish is less a menu option than a 'must-have,' though you can choose between cod, perch, or walleye. Oh, and potato pancakes are also mandatory: *no potato salad*. Right, Cody? Becky?" The kids nodded happily.

"Sounds good to me," said Josh with an eager look in his eye. "I'll have what you and Dr. Osborne have."

"Good," said Lew, "now that we have that settled, tell us what you do, Mr. Garner."

"Sure, but only if you call me 'Josh,'" said Josh with a smile. "Call me 'Mister' and I won't know who you're talking to. I'm an investigative reporter, Chief Ferris. I work for a news team that syndicates stories on state or national issues across the country. Mallory and I met when I was covering a data security breach affecting a financial institution in Chicago, which was one of her firm's clients. . . ."

Before he could say more, a surge in the noise level caused everyone at the table to look toward the front of the restaurant. A lanky figure in khaki cargo shorts and a black T-shirt emblazoned with neon green letters reading EXCITEMENT, ROMANCE AND LIVE BAIT: FISHING WITH RAY was ambling their way. At least he was headed in their direction before he kept stopping to chat at one table after another—so many times that Suzanne rolled her eyes at her mother.

"Honestly, is there anyone in Loon Lake Ray Pradt *doesn't* know?" asked Suzanne of everyone seated around her.

"If there is, I haven't met 'em," said Lew, buttering a roll.

Mallory, watching the man on whom she'd had a crush for years before they segued from an ill-advised intimacy into a friendship bordered with respect, understanding, and a large dose of self-deprecating humor, said to Josh, "Get ready. Ray is our neighbor at the lake and one of my dad's closest friends. He considers himself an expert on muskies, women, and the best weed on the market. Right, Dad?"

"Come on now," warned Osborne, throwing a glance toward Lew.

---

Mallory shrugged. She had been kidding, as she was well aware that while Ray might appear overly fond of cannabis, he was, in fact, a trusted source who kept Lew and the Loon Lake Police aware of changes in drug use among the people he knew: people who lived down roads with no fire numbers, people with no tax IDs, people who were the first to know when something new, exciting, and lethal became available. Whenever variations of dangerous drugs were introduced to the northwoods, Ray was often the first with an anonymous tip for law enforcement.

Did her father know that Ray was a key source for Lew? Mallory wasn't sure, but she had decided long ago to keep that information to herself. More important was that Ray had been instrumental in introducing Osborne—and herself—to the meetings held weekly behind the door with the coffeepot on the window. She had no intention of jeopardizing a friendship that had saved both their lives.

---

"Well, well, Suzanne, how are you? Haven't seen you in ages," said Ray, searching for space under the table for his grasshopper legs, "and you know Mallory, right? You heard about her new job? She's a Walmart greeter."

"Thank you, Mr. Pradt." Mallory did her best to sound wounded, but the twinkle in her eye gave her away. "Like you to meet my friend Josh Garner. He's hoping you might have room in your boat tomorrow to show him some muskie water."

Ray gave Josh a long look. "Maybe . . . but I don't think you'll need a fishing license, guy."

"Why not?" Josh looked confused.

"If you're under twelve—"

"Oh, for Pete's sake, Ray. Just shut up." Mallory tried to sound lighthearted, but she was irritated. Definitely irritated.

Listening to their banter, Osborne saw his friend give a quick glance down toward his phone, a worried glance that vanished the minute he looked up. Osborne made a mental note to check with him after dinner. So seldom did Ray worry about anything that Osborne wondered if one of his parents might be ill.

A bare male arm appeared without warning, draping itself across Mallory's shoulders. The owner of the arm bent over to nuzzle her ear even as Mallory twisted away. "Stop it, Bill," she said, grimacing. "Jeez Louise, you're like a human mosquito. A *married* human mosquito might I add."

"Aw, you're no fun," said the intruder with an eager smile as he nodded at everyone seated at the table. "Just trying to be social. Hey, Doc, Chief Ferris . . . So, Mal honey, when did you get back in town?"

The man named Bill continued to squeeze Mallory's shoulder while ignoring Josh seated next to her. Watching the proceedings, Osborne waited for Bill to get the message and move on, which couldn't happen soon enough for Osborne.

Bill Kimble was notorious for paying too much attention

to women, a habit he'd had since he was a teenager, a habit Osborne and his staff, which had included Bunny, the receptionist, and Miriam, the dental hygienist—knew too well. The problem was that Osborne's dental clinic had been located next door to Bill's father's real estate office.

This precipitated a daily ritual of teenage Bill stopping by the clinic after dropping off athletic gear he was too lazy to carry home or hitting his dad up for cash. At the time Bunny was an attractive blonde in her midforties who was skilled at entertaining the young guy for five minutes then shooing him out the door.

"I swear that kid was born a ladies' man," she once exclaimed to Osborne, sounding flattered but exasperated. While most men grow out of the flirting stage after marriage, Bill never matured past flirting, developing instead into a notorious womanizer.

Genetics made it easy for him: he was born good-looking, a natural athlete who played football one semester for the University of Wisconsin and was gifted with a natural, friendly charisma that made him both "a guy's guy" and a heartthrob to too many ladies.

Yes, he married his high school sweetheart, Evelyn Martin, who had been the prettiest girl in the school, and, yes, his parents died early in a car accident, leaving him millions of dollars in prime real estate—adding to his charm. That he was running through the money ridiculously fast and serially violating his marriage vows only made him more attractive to the lovely, cold, and calculating. One of these days, Osborne liked to think, the jerk would find himself way out of his league. But it hadn't happened yet.

After stroking Mallory's shoulder a minute too long, Bill turned his attention to Suzanne. She was ready and cut him off with an abrupt comment that she had just heard he'd lost money on a real estate investment in her hometown of Green Bay.

"Is that true?" she asked, feigning disbelief. Bill looked uncomfortable, waved good-bye to everyone, and slunk off.

Ray, watching him go, turned to Suzanne and said, "You know to be careful around that bastard, don't you?" Suzanne nodded with an expression on her face that implied she was well informed.

"Mallory Osborne." A loud female voice pierced the buzz of the room.

Looking up, Mallory met the eyes of a woman she had hoped never to see again.

# CHAPTER FIVE

The astonishment on Mallory's face caused Osborne to look around for the source. A tall spider of a woman loomed over his daughter. Osborne had to blink twice to be sure he was seeing only two long, bony arms—arms that the woman held akimbo on her hips as if she were giving orders.

"Oh my gosh, Judy, how long has it been?" asked Mallory as she pushed back her chair to stand and embrace the woman.

"Seventeen years to be exact, and the name these days is *Judith*. Different last name, too—Kerr. But there's no Mr. Kerr. He's history." The woman gave a tight smile as she emphasized the correct pronunciation of her first name.

It wasn't until he heard the querulous edge in the voice that it dawned on him: he was looking at someone who, along with her mother, had lived next door to him back when he and Mary Lee and their girls had lived in town. This was little Judy Kopicuski. Chubby little Judy Kopicuski. She may have dropped the baby fat, but she'd clearly held on to the whine-like voice of a constant complainer, a trait she shared with her late mother.

Had she married to rid herself of a four-syllable last

name? Or in an attempt to improve her mood? Osborne chided himself for being so critical.

As he listened to the exclamations being shared by the former childhood friends, he hoped their excitement at finding each other wouldn't go on too long, since a waitress had finally shown up to take their orders. He caught Lew's eye and could see she was thinking the same thing. She must have given up because she motioned for the waitress to go ahead and take the kids' orders.

". . . and where have you been all these years?" Mallory was asking. "I don't remember seeing you at our class reunion five years ago and I missed this year's gathering of our classmates."

"I made the recent class reunion, but that's the very first one I've been to," said Judith. "These past few years I've been out of the country. Until a month ago I was working in military intelligence at the highest level in the federal government. But"—again the grim smile—"right now I'm taking three months off while I change jobs. . . ."

"Sounds impressive," said Mallory. "But you were always a smart kid. Can I ask what's next or is that top secret?"

Osborne knew his daughter well enough to spot the irony hiding in her question, which a casual listener would find flattering. He kept his smile to himself.

"Same old story for those of us who do well in the spook biz," Judith was saying with an airy toss of her head. "Bottom line? I'm being dragged into the private sector. *Dragged*." She grimaced as she spoke. "But when you've been offered over a million bucks for a year's work, it's tough to resist. For the moment, though, I'm planning to enjoy a three-month hiatus.

Or as I told my new bosses: 'This girl is taking the summer off, goddammit.' " Again the tight smile.

As she spoke Osborne recalled that even as he had often felt sorry for her as a kid, he had found her difficult to like. Based on what he was hearing now, he was pretty sure he wasn't going to like her as an adult, either.

"But enough about me," said Judith. "How about you, Mallory, what are you doing? I didn't know you were back in Loon Lake." No one listening was going to miss the condescension in her voice.

"Hey, she has a *great* job," said Ray, his voice booming across the table from where he had been listening to every word. "She's a Walmart greeter."

"Really." Judith oozed sympathy.

"No," said Mallory, spitting out the word. "Honestly, Ray, that joke's getting old." She threw a dirty look across the table. "Don't listen to goofball over there," she said. "He thinks he's funny." She made a face in Ray's direction before turning back to Judith.

"I am *not* living in Loon Lake. Just here for a visit with my dad. I live in Chicago, where I'm VP of a public relations firm that has offices in New York, San Francisco, and Los Angeles. Coincidentally, Judith, our client list includes several high-tech companies that specialize in cybersecurity, which makes me wonder what firm you're joining? Who knows? Could be a client of ours. . . ."

"Oh, I can't say anything yet," said Judith, adopting a haughty tone. "The work I do is all very top drawer. In fact, we may have to keep my role confidential."

With that, Josh, who had been listening intently to the

two women, stood up and reached to shake Judith's hand. After introducing himself, he said, "Excuse me for interrupting but were you with the NSA or the CIA? I've covered both agencies in my work and I'm familiar with quite a few of the experts. . . ."

Judith stared at him for a long moment before saying, "The NSA, but I cannot share details, not even names. Sorry." She turned back toward Mallory, leaving Josh standing.

After a brief pause, he got the hint and sat down.

As he listened to the women and Josh, Osborne couldn't help but wonder how it was he was hearing the acronym NSA twice in one day—and in Loon Lake, a town so far from Washington, D.C., that most people wouldn't know what NSA stood for.

"Judith, if I weren't here for such a short time, I would suggest we get together," said Mallory. "Why don't I let you know ahead of time when I'll be back and we can catch up?"

"Good idea," said Judith. "By the way," she added, "do you see quite a bit of Bill Kimble?"

"Not really," said Mallory, sounding taken aback by the question. "He's married to Evie Martin, you know."

"I guess I did know that," said Judith in a spritely tone. "Well, yes, let's get together. I'll give you a call or a text."

"Sure, let me give you my number for your phone," said Mallory. After exchanging numbers, Judith walked around the table to stand next to Ray. "You look familiar. Aren't you one of the Pradt kids?"

"Yep," said Ray, "I'm Ray, the one who never grew up. I was a year behind you in school."

"Of course," said Judith, "and are you a doctor or a lawyer like your siblings?"

"Nope," said Ray. He got to his feet, grabbed the front of his T-shirt, and held it so she could read the slogan. "This is me," he said, "'Excitement, Romance and Live Bait: Fishing with Ray.' Just your standard-issue fishing guide."

Looking him up and down, Judith said in a coy tone, "Really? You don't look too standard issue to me. Maybe I should get your number, too?"

"If you're looking to fish? By all means," said Ray. "I'm your man in the boat for muskie, bass, or walleye." With that, he gave her his phone number and watched as she punched it into her phone.

When she had finished, Judith slipped her phone into a purse slung over her shoulder and said, "One thing I've been planning to do while I'm up here is learn how to fish. Never did as a kid. So I'll definitely give you a call. Can I assume you rent fishing gear?"

"I have everything you'll need."

Mallory snorted, and it was Ray's turn to look irritated. But only for a second.

"Anyone mind if we order now?" asked Lew, beckoning toward the waitress, who'd been waiting patiently.

"Oh, I am so sorry. Please, people, order," said Judith. "I'll be calling you," she said, pointing an index finger at Ray before turning to walk off into the dining room.

Mallory waited to be sure she was out of earshot before saying, "That was a surprise. Sorry, everyone, for holding up our dinner."

"Wasn't your fault," said Josh. "We all know that a 'top

drawer' person has to come first. Right?" He grinned. "An old friend, I take it?"

"Well, not exactly a friend," said Mallory. "I'll tell you more later."

Osborne, in spite of his initial shock at Josh's apparent youth, began to reconsider. He just might like the young man after all.

# CHAPTER SIX

Osborne lingered so he could walk out of the restaurant behind Ray. Once they were on the sidewalk, he pulled Ray aside. "What's wrong? Are your parents okay? You seemed preoccupied all through dinner."

"Everyone in my family is fine," said Ray, his eyes serious. "It's Lillian Curran. She called me two days ago and asked me to drop by today with a dozen bluegills. She said she was planning to eat half and freeze half. But when I went by her house, no one was home, and, well, Doc, that's odd. So I went by her place once more before coming here but she was still gone."

"C'mon, Ray, our old friend Lillian is as eccentric as they come. You know that," said Osborne. "How about last fall when she took off without telling a single soul—not even the post office—that she was flying to a Buddhist monastery on top of some mountain in Japan for a month? Now *that's* odd."

Ray managed a smile. "True. She is a character, for sure."

"That's an understatement," said Osborne, who knew the elderly lawyer well.

Lillian Curran had been a patient of his for over a decade. She was a retired criminal defense lawyer who became famous early in her career for defending two young brothers who had kidnapped the daughter of a lumber baron. After they were caught—and they had not harmed the young woman—Lillian took on their defense in hopes of saving them from life in prison or a death penalty.

"I talked to those boys, Doc," she had told Osborne, "and I could tell that growing up, they had never gotten a break. Sure they did wrong, really wrong. But I knew they could be rehabilitated.

"Their only hope was to be represented by a woman— back in the day, that fact alone would surprise people. Who could better persuade a jury that they were not the devil incarnate? And that girl they kidnapped? Her testimony about how kind they had been to her—well, I didn't have to say much more."

When Lillian won twenty-year sentences for the boys, she won national news. She also made sure that while they were imprisoned, they got trained to work on dairy farms and when they were released in their early forties, she helped them get jobs.

"I did the right thing, Doc," she told Osborne. "They worked hard, they raised families, and they made me proud." The only problem from Lillian's point of view was that she outlived them.

After retiring from the bar, Lillian had moved to a small cottage on the western shore of Loon Lake where she became an avid birder and an outspoken—to put it mildly—advocate for birds of prey.

Owls were her passion. But she was so fervent a birder that she refused to let other owl enthusiasts know where and when they might observe "her" birds. Nor did she let the definition of "private property" deter her dedication to observing the denizens of the dark. More than once she had been threatened with a lawsuit for trespassing on private land.

"You're right, of course," said Ray. "I guess what bothers me is that she *loves* bluegills. And this is Friday, her favorite night to have fish. But she is ninety years old after all, Doc. Maybe . . ."

"Why don't we do this," said Osborne. "Lew is taking the weekend off with her daughter and little Becky. Let's talk to Lew right now and see if she can arrange for whoever is on duty tonight to check Lillian's house. If her car is in the drive, you'll know she's fine. Sound like a good idea?"

"Yes," said Ray, "I'll feel better if we do that."

On the drive home, as Cody nodded off beside him, Osborne mulled over the surprise appearance of Judith Kerr, a tall and very thin Judith. He couldn't erase the image he had from when she was a youngster: chubby and sullen. Though he had never warmed to her as a child, he had felt sorry for her. Judy, as they called her then, did not grow up in a happy home.

---

Lydia Kopicuski, her mother, was a dark-haired woman with permanent black circles under her eyes, a woman who rarely smiled. Perhaps for good reason. Lydia's first husband had announced one evening he was going out to buy cigarettes and never returned. Little Judy was four the year her dad left.

That may not have been the worst event, however. Lydia

had been a member of Mary Lee's bridge group, and when the group learned that she would be divorced, they informed Lydia she was no longer welcome: "We don't believe in divorce, Lydia," they had said, as if the breakup of her marriage was all Lydia's fault.

Osborne suspected the real reason was that the bridge ladies didn't want their husbands getting any ideas. Though he knew better than to voice his opinion to his late wife, it gave him one more reason to dislike her friends—along with their petty gossip about nonmembers of their clique and their emphasis on clothes, furniture, and anything else money could buy. One woman who lost her home when her husband's car repair business went bankrupt was also ostracized: "We don't see an apartment as being large enough for our two tables for bridge *and* luncheon," he remembered hearing one of them say.

Osborne, knowing better than to criticize the bridge group's decisions and risk a shrill confrontation with Mary Lee, chose instead to escape to his dental practice and muskie boat. Years later, when it became the norm for young people to live together before marriage, he was envious. If only he had known *before* his wedding what he learned soon after . . . ah, well, he wasn't alone.

While he would not accuse all the members of the bridge group of a lack of compassion, he heard enough from the other husbands to know that their marriages weren't overflowing with mutual appreciation, either. Perhaps that was why he let Mary Lee run their lives: not even the buddies with whom he fished had a storybook marriage.

After he moved his family into the big new house on

Loon Lake, he often thought of Lydia and little Judy. Though Lydia remarried a few years after her divorce, their lives took another tragic turn. That husband left, too—committing suicide at his hunting shack.

More than once Osborne would wonder what it was about that hollow-eyed woman that doomed her and her daughter to such a sad existence. Whatever it was, Judith as a teenager behaved in alarming ways.

One of the worst was when, at the age of fifteen, Judith went to the high school principal and accused Mallory of cheating on an English test. Not just any test but one of three used to determine placement in AP English their senior year. For Mallory, who was hoping to get into Northwestern University, that placement was crucial.

Osborne and Mary Lee confronted their daughter, who swore she had done no such thing. Within twenty-four hours, the English teacher came to her defense, pointing out that it had been "an open-book test and impossible to cheat on." End of story. But why did Judith accuse Mallory? Was it her mother's idea? Retribution for the bridge group's insult?

Also during those years, Osborne heard vague rumors of promiscuous behavior, of stealing from lockers, and the destruction of other girls' purses and backpacks. Whenever he heard the rumors, Osborne thought of the hollow-eyed woman who had driven two men to extremes. What had she done to her daughter?

---

After Osborne tucked Cody into bed with a promise of morning fishing in the Alumacraft, he climbed into his own bed, ready to read a few more pages of *A River Runs Through It*. No sooner had he opened the book than his cell phone rang.

"She's not home yet, Doc," said Ray. "I just got back from meeting Officer Donovan at Lillian's place. Her car was gone, and the house was locked.

"Doc, I'm worried. Before I got back into my truck and while it was still light out, I could see that garden of hers with the Japanese grasses and all those stone Buddhas she tucks in everywhere. And it was too quiet, y'know? Waaay too quiet. Okay, I'll shut up. Sorry to bother you."

Ray hung up, and Osborne lay in bed thinking. Too quiet is right, but more important—who forgets fresh bluegills from Ray?

# CHAPTER SEVEN

A t four in the morning, Lew's beeper and cell phone went off simultaneously. Shooting up onto her elbows as she grabbed the cell phone, she blinked, struggling to see the screen in the dim light. It was the officer she trusted: Todd Donovan.

Unlike Roger Adamczyk, Donovan, who was her second-in-command, never overreacted. Burglaries, domestic confrontations, even recalcitrant drunks he would handle without calling her unless absolutely necessary. And "necessary" was likely to be serious, such as needing a search warrant.

The beeper signal was from the sheriff's department. Never a good sign. Did that mean Todd needed backup?

The county sheriff and his deputies were responsible for law enforcement throughout the county, while the Loon Lake Police Department was legally responsible for the town of Loon Lake only. Both were budgeted accordingly but often coordinated their efforts, as the Loon Lake Police Department had only three full-time police officers to help and protect Loon Lake's official population of 3,112. But while that small (fall, winter, spring) population might appear manageable, it was a population that soared to more than 20,000 from mid-June to late September thanks to an annual influx of summer residents and tourists. Hence Lew and her officers operated under orders to call for assistance when confronted or out-manned by trouble or tragedy during the busy summer months.

"Ferris here," said Lew as she answered the call on her cell phone. "Are you all right?"

"Chief," Todd replied, "I've got a double fatality on Spider Lake Road." The young officer's tone was curt. "Sorry to wake you but—"

"Do we know the victims?"

"Yes. It's John and Margo Powers, a business executive from Evanston, Illinois, and his wife. The sheriff's department called me after a neighbor complained of a dog barking all night. When I got no answer to their doorbell or knocking on the doors, I found a woman I assume is the wife in the kitchen, the husband in the garage. Both appear to have bullet wounds. This could be murder-suicide.

"And, yes, Chief, I did call the sheriff's switchboard for backup until I was sure there was no one else on the premises. Sorry to be calling at this hour."

"Never be sorry—be safe. Address?" Lew was half dressed and waving at her daughter, who was standing in the doorway with a question in her eyes.

"Sorry, Suzanne," said Lew in a loud whisper. She covered the phone with one hand while listening to Todd. When she had the address and ended the call, she turned to her daughter. "Sorry, Suzanne, you may need to find a sitter for Becky. I've got two fatalities to deal with. I'll call in when I know more." By the time she had finished talking, she was nearly out the door and running for her cruiser.

The woman in the kitchen was sprawled across a black and white tile floor, her head and upper body in a pool of blood so large that Lew knew she had not died instantly. Lew did not have to get close to see the left side of her jaw was torn away, exposing the cheek muscles.

The husband had been killed as he was getting out of his Range Rover in the garage, where he lay facedown across the driver's seat of the car. She had a hunch he had been shot multiple times, but that was information she would have to wait for the Wausau boys from the crime lab to confirm.

Standing alongside Officer Donovan, Lew called the coroner's home number, figuring he would be asleep and, knowing Ed Pecore's predilection for way too many vodka tonics at bedtime, she planned to let it ring forever if she had to. To her surprise, his wife answered instantly.

"Oh, Chief Ferris, I thought you were at the hospital," she said. "I had to rush Ed to the emergency room, and they're operating now—burst appendix. I just ran home to grab a few things—"

"Oh," said Lew, trying to sound concerned in spite of being secretly relieved. "Please keep me posted. I hope he does okay." She didn't add that people pickled in alcohol could have serious health issues during surgery. Instead, she called the one person she knew she could deputize to be a reliable acting coroner: Dr. Paul Osborne.

"Sorry, Doc," said Lew to the drowsy voice on the phone. "I have two fatalities over on Spider Lake. Not sure if murder-suicide or a double homicide, but what I am sure of is that Pecore is out of commission with a burst appendix. I'm afraid I need your help."

As Osborne sat up in bed, he reached over to calm Mike, his black Lab, who thought a human sitting up meant time to chase chipmunks. "I'll need to wake Cody," said Osborne. "His parents texted late last night that they're home, so I can drop him off on my way over. And do we have any idea who the victims are? Tourists renting the cottage?"

"I know exactly who they are," said Lew. "It's John Powers from Evanston, Illinois. He's a wealthy industrialist and he and his wife built this place recently. Moved in several months ago. At least that's what a neighbor told me."

"I've heard that name," said Osborne. "The Powers name is on every steel silo you see on farms across the Midwest. John Powers is the third generation to run the company, and he and his wife have vacationed up here for years. Three years ago I treated his wife for a broken tooth that required a crown. If I remember right, her name is Margo."

"Good memory, Doc. Boy, if there's a chance you might have a dental chart for her in those old files of yours—"

"I'll check later, let me get going here. I imagine you'll be putting in a call to the Wausau boys?" he asked, referring to the Wausau Crime Lab, which Loon Lake law enforcement relied on—and funded—for assistance with homicides, deaths from unknown circumstances, and other felony investigations that might require high-tech expertise and equipment.

"Yep, that'll make my morning," said Lew, her tone dry. "But first, I have to call in to his firm and hope the offices aren't closed on the weekend. We'll need someone official up here to ID the bodies. Oh, hey, got a call coming in, Doc. That may be the crime lab."

———

After dropping off a half-awake eight-year-old, Osborne sped out to Spider Lake, which was twenty minutes out of town but still within Lew's jurisdiction. She and Officer Donovan were waiting on the screened-in porch of the large lake home, which appeared to be the size of a small resort rather than a private residence.

Osborne followed Lew into the kitchen where the wife's body lay. After slipping protective covers on his shoes, he was able to avoid disturbing the pool of blood around the body while getting close enough to confirm there was no pulse.

As he stared at what remained of the woman's face, he recalled seeing her three years ago, the summer before he closed his office. He had been struck by her beauty: she'd had large, violet eyes, a halo of pale blond hair, and a quiet, elegant presence. He had liked her. A frisson of sorrow swept across his heart.

Watching Osborne as he stared down at the still figure, Lew said, "I reached one of the husband's colleagues who said he'd been pulling an all-nighter at their offices and saw my call come in.

"He also said the company is in the middle of two very contentious lawsuits—so contentious that Powers recently received calls and emails threatening the personal safety of him and his wife. The threats were alarming enough that the company has been paying for extra security around the Powers home down in Evanston. They thought he would be safe up here, as he's been involved in legal disputes for years and never had any individual intrude on his time when he was away from the city."

Osborne followed Lew to the garage where the husband, hair prematurely white, appeared to also have been shot from behind. It was easy to see he was tall and tanned, as his legs were exposed below a pair of plaid golf shorts. The body was lying facedown, sprawled half in and half out of a white Range Rover.

After Osborne felt for the signs of life he knew he wouldn't find, he surmised that Powers may have been returning from an evening of golf with friends. If so that might help the crime scene experts out of the Wausau Crime Lab to determine an approximate time of death.

He turned to Lew, who was on her cell phone and grimacing. He knew why: she was waiting to speak to the director of the Wausau Crime Lab. This could turn ugly. . . .

# CHAPTER EIGHT

Y ou know the protocol," said the male voice on the phone, "you have to send me a written request that specifies exactly what is needed from the Wausau Crime Lab. Nothing unreasonable about this, Lewellyn." He pointedly did not call her Chief Ferris.

Lew recognized the whiny tone belonging to Doug Jesperson, a man she preferred to call "the weasel." Formerly director of the Wausau Crime Lab, "the weasel" was technically retired but would fill in whenever the current director was on vacation.

On this early Saturday morning Lew was chagrined to find the director was on weekend leave for a family wedding. On hearing that news, she threw a look of exasperation at Osborne: all right, time to work the weasel.

"Yes, I know the protocol," said Lew, keeping her voice measured, "but I also know it is being revised due to all the advances in DNA—especially since we now know that delays of hours, even minutes, can destroy some trace evidence. Plus, to be frank, Doug, I don't know enough about the latest DNA research to know what to ask for. And, Doug," she said, pushing her luck but determined to rely on fact, "I happen to know you didn't hold Sheriff Richards responsible for following protocol when he found those two dead hunters last Easter—"

"He's a *sheriff*," said Jesperson, implying his opinion of town police versus county sheriffs.

Lew held her tongue, knowing the issue at hand was not the "protocol"—it was the fact that the jerk on the other phone did not hide his bias against women in law enforcement. Lewellyn Ferris's promotion to chief of the Loon Lake Police by the town's City Council still rankled him, and he never hesitated to let her know it.

At least today, he wasn't holding her hostage to his usual litany of dirty jokes. Maybe it was too early in the morning to manage that. Instead, he started to repeat, "Our crime lab protocol requires you to write and fax in or email a formal request detailing the circumstances of the alleged—"

"I know the protocol," said Lew, interrupting. "What I need to know is if Bruce Peters is available this morning. Can you confirm that?" Again she kept her voice level and her fingers crossed.

Silence. "My team is working up the protocol," she lied to break the silence.

"All right," said the weasel a long two minutes later. "Looks like I got Peters on the line . . . I'm putting him through."

"Thank you." Lew tried not to sound as relieved as she felt. Whew. She had begun to worry that she might have the weasel himself come up to handle the crime scene.

"Hey, Chief, you are interrupting my Saturday," said a cheerful voice. Bruce Peters. Finally, an ally at the crime lab. "How's it going up there on the big lakes? Afraid I'm committed to cleaning the garage unless you got a better idea—like one involving a fly rod or two? Got a new four-weight needs testing. . . . "

Lew chuckled. "Bruce, are you sure this won't endanger your marriage?"

"We can try." Lew imagined Bruce Peters's bushy eyebrows bouncing up and down as he teased. "Nah, Carrie understands—if I'm happy, she's happy."

"All kidding aside, we have a possible murder-suicide or maybe two individuals dead under questionable circumstances."

Quickly she laid out the scene at the Powers home, then said, "Doc Osborne has determined both parties are deceased from apparent bullet wounds. Officer Donovan established an entry and exit path when he answered a three a.m. neighbor's call that the family's dogs had been barking all night.

"I subsequently met Doc Osborne out on the road and, before entering the Powers home, we both wore covers on our shoes. I have taken care to view both bodies from the path set by Donovan so you should have a pristine crime scene."

"And the dogs? Please tell me they weren't in the house—"

"No, in a pen in the owners' backyard. I assume they were usually let in at night—but not last night, obviously."

"Good work," said Bruce, serious now. "I'll be there within an hour unless the 'copter is available. Address?" After Lew gave him that information, she asked, "Do you need me to write up the protocol?"

"Hell, no. Not if you agree to a little time in a trout stream sometime in the next couple days."

"Ooh, that's easy," said Lew with a smile so broad that Osborne and Officer Donovan, who had been listening to Lew's end of the conversation, chuckled together.

"Thank heavens," she said, rolling her eyes after saying thank you and a polite good-bye to the weasel, who had come back on the line for assurance that Bruce would handle the case.

Off the phone, she turned to Officer Donovan. "You have had a long night, Todd," she said. "I've got this covered, so hurry home and get some sleep. You can write up your report later."

Lew's cell phone beeped. It was Bruce. "Hey, Chief, got the 'copter and loading gear right now, but any chance my good buddy Ray is available for photos this morning? Both our guys are working a drug bust in Merrill."

"I'll check with him right now," said Lew.

"Yeah? Well take care, you don't want to wake the lady," said Bruce, who made no secret of his envy of Ray's talent for securing female companionship.

———

Bruce Peters might be a forensic scientist steeped in chemistry, computers, physics, and other scientific data sources, but not even his happy marriage kept him from puzzling over male/female psychology. In other words, he couldn't help wondering what might have been had he been born with Ray's good looks, long legs, auburn curls, and easy way around women.

Hearing Bruce try to dissect why women were attracted to the fishing guide who was his same age and had significantly fewer financial resources, Lew had to shake her head. All the science in the world couldn't answer that. Maybe it was as simple as this: some men just never grow up. And some women find that charming.

———————

Just as she was ready to give Osborne's neighbor a wake-up call, her cell phone rang. "Yes, Officer Adamczyk, what's up?" said Lew, hoping Roger was calling about something more important than a vandalized trash can.

"Chief, just letting you know I'm booking three juveniles this morning for vandalism on the Loon Lake channels. There was a beer party out on the island last night and three of the jokers moved the buoy markers."

"Any accidents?" Lew cringed as she asked the question. The morning was already too busy.

"Nothing major, Chief. Had a call from a fisherman out early this morning whose prop hit that big boulder just off the point. He fishes that area regularly, so he knew right away that the buoys had been tampered with.

"When I pulled up to the landing to meet him, we found three male juveniles asleep in a pickup registered to one kid's parents. Found one of the buoys in the bed of the truck, too, so I know it was them. Not sure what they did with the rest of the buoys. The juveniles are still under the influence, if you know what I mean."

"Thank goodness they weren't driving," said Lew.

"I know," said Roger, "but who do I call to get marker buoys back where they belong before we have a serious accident?"

"Hold on," said Lew. She looked at Osborne, saying, "Doc, Roger said some kids have moved the marker buoys on the

Loon Lake channels. Should he call the DNR to be sure the buoys are anchored where they belong? Or someone else?"

"The lake association has two men who take care of that," said Osborne. "Tell Roger to call Chuck Stafford. He's the association president and he'll know who to reach."

Lew passed on the message then said, "Take those boys to the station. They need to understand how serious that is. Call their parents and have them come in, too." She could hear Roger hesitate, and for the umpteenth time she felt the frustration of working with the razzbonya.

---

Roger Adamczyk had been drifting along in a mediocre career selling life insurance when he spotted a job posting for a police officer for the Loon Lake Police Department. Thinking that job had to be an easy route to a state pension and involved little more than giving out parking tickets and arresting drunk drivers—many of whom were likely to be his former clients—he applied for the training and, being one of the few applicants who tested drug free, was accepted.

This was before Lewellyn Ferris had been made chief of the department, so she inherited Officer Adamcyzk, likely one of the laziest and most mild-mannered law enforcement professionals she had ever expected to encounter, much less manage. But he was "a lifer," so there was little she could do to change things.

However, a rise in property values coupled with a constant influx of drugs changed life in the northwoods. Break-ins and drug busts strained the resources of Loon Lake's modest law enforcement team. Who cared about parking tickets when a local bar turned out to be headquarters for a million-dollar money-laundering scheme? And so it was that poor Officer Adamczyk now woke up on many mornings wondering, What was I thinking?—before heading out to face another challenging day.

———

At the moment, Lew knew, he would gladly trade checking parking meters for confronting three hungover teenage boys and their upset parents.

"Officer Adamczyk, did you hear me?" asked Lew. "Ask Dispatch to call the boys' parents and tell them to meet you at the station. You don't need to arrest those kids, but they need a good talking to. Got it?"

Still the hesitation.

"Roger," she said, tightening her voice, "are you in uniform?"

"Of course."

"You are the authority. Now, please, these are badly behaving teenage boys, not murderous drug dealers. Please take care of the situation. I have my hands full with a crime scene. The Wausau boys are set to arrive any moment and my weekend is gone. Will you *please* just do your job?"

# CHAPTER NINE

**R**ay was reaching into the refrigerator for a carton of eggs when his cell phone rang. As he answered he glanced out the window facing the lake. "Good morning, Chief Ferris—up for some early morning fishing?"

He heard Lew snort and was about to chuckle at his own joke when he was surprised to see the back of a tall blond-haired woman walking across the clearing in front of his house trailer. She was headed in the direction of the dock where his boat was moored.

He was befuddled: What on earth? At six in the morning?

He tried his best to listen as Lew gave him hurried directions to grab his cameras and meet up with her at an address on Spider Lake Road, but he continued to keep his eyes on the figure walking out onto his dock.

"Bruce is arriving any moment," Lew was saying after describing the grim scene that Ray would have to capture on film. "He said to tell you he's sorry if you have a guide job you have to cancel, but the crime lab's photographers are busy with a major drug bust. So, Ray, can you do this? This is a major case—"

"I'll be there ASAP," said Ray as he stepped through the

mouth of the neon-green muskie painted around the front door of his house trailer.

Still in his boxer shorts and bare-chested, he was determined to intercept the idiot female—probably some crazed early-morning jogger from the cities—before she messed with any of his priceless fishing gear. Wouldn't be the first time. And he had learned the hard way not to be polite with people who assumed that all lake shoreline was public access.

The only female Ray let close to his rods and reels and tackle without his close supervision was Osborne's granddaughter, Mason. And she was twelve years old with dark hair. The blonde walking along the dock with her back to him was not a brunette—and definitely not twelve years old, either.

"Hey, you," was all he managed to holler before she turned around.

The intruder was Judith Kerr, the woman he'd observed talking to Mallory at the restaurant the night before, the woman who seemed so curious about Bill Kimble. "You're an early riser," was all he could manage.

"I wanted to be first in line to book you for a day of fishing. I need to learn how to catch a muskie," she said with a bright smile.

"And I'd love to talk to you about it," said Ray, grabbing her by the elbow and walking her off his dock. "But I'm in a hurry to be somewhere right now. Call me later and we'll set something up."

As they reached the clearing in front of his trailer, he said, "Wait here while I grab you one of my business cards." He walked over to where he had parked his blue pickup. "I got a card in my glove compartment."

Relieved that she was following orders, he reached for a card, then reconsidered and handed her two, and did his best to wave her good-bye. She had parked her black SUV right behind his truck, which annoyed him. "Say, you've got to move that car right away, okay? I'm in a hurry—"

"Dressed like that?" she asked him with a smile. She didn't appear to be ready to move as quickly as he needed.

"Look, I have an emergency. Please move your car." Ray started back toward his front door.

"Got it," she said climbing into her car. "Has anyone ever told you you're cute when you're rude?"

Ray closed his eyes in frustration. "I am sorry but this is—"

"I know, I know, an emergency," she said. "I'm leaving." She stopped suddenly. "One more thing—I think you know Bill Kimble?"

"Yeah, he's a local. Everyone knows everyone around here." Turning his back to signal the end of the conversation, Ray pulled open the screen door.

"Check your calendar for when I call you. I want to give him a day of fishing with you as a birthday gift."

"Sure." Ray slammed the door shut, exhaled, and raced to finish dressing. Jeez Louise, he thought. What a way to start a day.

―――――――

After conferring with Lew and Bruce, Ray started shooting at the juncture of the town road and the Powerses' driveway before moving forward until he reached the paved stone walkway into the house. Following the entrance and exit path that had been established by Officer Donovan, he moved closer and closer to the victims, taking care to shoot the surrounding area in case Bruce's forensic team needed to examine floors, walls, and furniture.

"Whoa," he said to Lew while taking a short break, "what do you think? A burglary gone bad?"

Lew shrugged. "No idea yet. The only news I have so far is that the victim, John Powers, had a few business enemies. Even so, this is pretty extreme. His business partner and company lawyer are flying up in a private plane, getting here late this morning. We may know more then."

"You know, Chief Ferris," said Ray, "I hate to bring this up, but I am still very worried about Lillian Curran. I'll swing by her place later but she wasn't home late last night. . . ."

Lew, distracted by Bruce Peters's arrival, was only half-listening to what he was saying. Ray could see that she had her hands full. He made a mental note to peer into Lillian's windows the next time he checked her house.

————————

The Powerses were so well known that once word had leaked out of their unexplained deaths, the Chicago city and business media rushed to cover the story. The news spread so quickly that the private plane carrying the executive and lawyer from the Powers company reached the home on Spider Lake simultaneously with a van belonging to a television crew and a rental car driven by a financial reporter from the *Chicago Tribune*. The vehicles narrowly missed colliding at the entrance to the drive leading to the Powers residence.

After introducing himself to Lew, the lawyer for the company said, "Chief Ferris, we have a situation here that could alarm our shareholders if this news isn't handled right. Do you have a problem making a statement to the press but letting us deal with detailed information about the family and the company?"

"Maybe," said Lew. "I would appreciate speaking with you two before you make statements so that no information is released that might jeopardize our investigation. Also, you must clear this with that gentleman there"—she pointed to Bruce Peters—"he is the forensic expert from the Wausau Crime Lab and the investigation is under his command. Clear every detail with both Bruce and myself. And, please, the less I have to deal with the media, the better.

"If you're saying you think the death of Mr. Powers and his wife are related to his business activities, please be aware that we haven't ruled out that this could be a murder-suicide."

The lawyer paused before speaking then said, "I won't be surprised if both people weren't killed by someone connected to one of John's lawsuits. Could be someone from outside the United States. For that reason, we're already in contact with the FBI."

"No doubt they have more resources than we do," said Lew, "but, again, please keep our Wausau boys in the loop."

---

It was shortly before midnight when Lew walked into her living room off the kitchen to find Suzanne curled up on the leather sofa, scanning her cell phone.

She looked up as Lew flopped down beside her. "Hey, Mom, thanks for giving me a call earlier or I would have been worried about you. Becky is sound asleep—I was able to bring her to the wedding. Lots of young kids were there and she had a good time."

"I am so sorry," said Lew. "I had been looking forward to having her help me plant tomatoes, darn."

"She was, too, but we have to leave early in the morning. I have a business to run, y'know."

"I know," said Lew, kissing her daughter on the forehead. "It's been good to see you guys, though."

"One thing, Mom . . ." As she spoke, Suzanne's forehead wrinkled and she scrunched her eyes. "I'm wondering if I maybe said the wrong thing last night at dinner."

"What do you mean? I don't remember you saying anything, or behaving any other way than pleasant. Why?"

"I had two voice mails on my cell from that Bill Kimble—wanting me to meet him for coffee. Isn't he married?"

"Very much so, I believe. Ray doesn't care for the guy. Maybe he's just a flirt and remembers you from back in the Boom Bay era?"

Suzanne sighed and shook her head. "That's awful. I hate that. I left him a voice mail saying I'm very involved with someone else and not interested. Did not hear anything after that, thank goodness."

———

It was the year that Lew left her husband and was working as a secretary at the paper mill. She didn't have the money for Suzanne to go to college, so Suzanne took a year to work before enrolling. She was fortunate to find a job that paid very well, even if it was short on prestige: she worked as a pole dancer at the notorious Boom Bay Bar.

Unknown to the patrons who applauded her and delivered generous tips, she had made an agreement with her mother before taking the job: Lew would be in the parking lot every night to pick her up after she finished her stint at the bar. The difficulty was that she finished her night's work at midnight and they lived twenty minutes away.

But Lew would show up for her mill job promptly at 8:00 a.m. the next morning and Suzanne would make enough money to enroll in college the next fall. After graduating with a degree in accounting, she worked for a short time for another firm before opening her own.

Today her business was flourishing and all the college loans had been paid. The only downside was Suzanne's brief marriage, which lasted only four years. Lew hated thinking it was her own poor judgment in *her* marriage that had influenced her daughter. But then she would look at Becky, her cheery granddaughter; her grandson, Jason, now in third grade and a star hockey player; and her busy, happy daughter—and give herself a pass.

---

"Let's figure Kimble's a creep and let it go," said Lew.

"So, Mom," said Suzanne, getting to her feet and pulling her robe around her, "I almost forgot to tell you that some woman stopped by just before dark asking for you."

"Oh? I wonder who that was," said Lew, mystified but too tired to care much. Probably Marge from next door. "What did she look like?"

"Short brown hair."

"That doesn't say much."

"Never saw her before. She didn't seem worried when I said you weren't here. She left right away."

Lew's curiosity trumped her fatigue: "What kind of car was she driving?"

"Mom, I have no idea. I was so happy to sit down after all day at Brenda's wedding, I'm afraid I didn't pay much attention. Sorry, but that's why you're in law enforcement and I'm an accountant."

"True," said Lew, giving her a hug. "I'm sure whoever it is will stop back. Has to be a friend anyway, since not that many people know where I live. Now head off to bed. I'm dead tired, too, but I'll make you coffee before you leave in the morning."

"Perfect, Mom. Good night."

Moments later all the women in the little red farmhouse were sound asleep.

# CHAPTER TEN

Ray drove into Lillian Curran's driveway, put his truck in park, and studied the small, dark house: no lights. He reached for a flashlight, got out of his truck, and walked up to the front door. He knocked, waited, and was not surprised when there was no answer.

Pushing through the hydrangea bush under the two front windows, he used the flashlight's strong beam to search the room behind the glass for signs of recent activity. No luck. He backed out and walked over to the other windows. This time he was looking into the dining room. No change from what he had seen the day before. He sighed and walked back to his truck.

Climbing into the truck, he paused, thinking. He couldn't get over a dark low sense that something wasn't right. He sighed again and backed out of the driveway.

───────────

Back in his house trailer, Ray closed the door to his darkroom and started to work with the photos he had shot for Bruce and his forensic team. It took until two in the morning before he was able to send off the final digitized sets with the promise he would deliver prints—color as well as black-and-white—early the next morning.

Then he fell into bed. During the night, he woke twice to thunder, then turned over to fall back asleep, hoping the skies would clear before Josh and Mallory arrived for a morning on his boat. He had promised to give Josh a lesson on casting the spinning rod that Josh had found in his late father's garage.

---

At 5:00 a.m. he delivered two sets of prints from the crime scene to the Loon Lake Police Department. Lew had not yet arrived but Marlaine, the night dispatcher, knew the drill: "Got 'em," she said, curt as always. "Chief's due any minute and they'll be on her desk."

Then he drove back to the lake, his heart a little lighter, since the air had cooled and that—plus the recent storms— might make for good fishing.

---

"If we're lucky, we got muskies on a feeding spree this morning," said Ray as he loaded gear into his boat. "Josh, here's lesson one," he said with a grin, "when you got wind plus weather changes, especially in the early summer—you got the best conditions for muskie fishing you can ask for."

"Is that based on science?" asked Josh as he reached back to give Mallory a hand into the boat.

"Experience," said Ray. "I'm probably the guy with the least amount of electronics and other gadgets on the lake but I've been fishing since I was seven years old, so I go with my gut. We had storms overnight and that is always a good sign."

"You gotta listen to him," said Mallory. "Ray may make grievous errors in other areas of his life but not in the boat. He's the man, Josh."

"Thank you, M," said Ray in a wry tone. After their brief fling a year earlier, he and Mallory had made their peace and settled into a comfortable, if sometimes too frank, friendship.

Mallory's eyes twinkled at his comment. The fact was she owed Ray: she had turned to him after a difficult divorce and during a time when she had begun to drink too much. Goofball though he was, Ray had listened, offering a perceptive take on the negative influences she'd experienced as the oldest daughter and the favorite of her late mother.

Mary Lee had been a woman determined to blame other people for her mistakes—especially her husband.

Mallory wasn't stupid. She had often wondered why her mother would refuse to take responsibility for errors as small as making bad purchases. But the day her mother said "If your father wasn't such a bad dentist, we could have moved to a big city where a dental practice would pay him much more money"—that was the moment when Mallory changed her perspective.

She knew from other dentists who were friends of her father's through his involvement with the Wisconsin Dental Society that her dad did fine work. He was well respected among his peers, more than one of whom went out of their way, when Osborne had taken the family along to attend "family night" during the Society's annual meeting, to mention what "an excellent dentist your dad is" to Mallory and her younger sister, Erin.

Most important, she knew why her father loved having his dental practice in the northwoods of Wisconsin.

On Wednesdays and Saturdays, as he climbed into his trusty fishing boat for an afternoon on the water, she could see the stress from the dental office (and from a tongue-lashing he may have just taken from Mary Lee) disappear from his eyes. And she knew he wasn't kidding (really) when he would joke (to the girls, not their mother) that "the reason a man like me practices dentistry is so I can afford to fish." And he would give them a wink, but she knew he meant it.

And she had commiserated with her younger sister over why their mother was so critical of their father: "I think they didn't know each other very well when they got married," Erin had said, by way of excusing their parents' personality mismatch.

Mallory had agreed, adding, "Yeah, and maybe 'cause his mother died when he was six, so he never grew up with a mom. Maybe that's why he didn't understand women very well when he first met Mom? Maybe because she was so pretty on the outside, he thought she would be good on the inside?"

The sisters were twelve and fourteen when they had held that amateur therapy session. But talking over their mother's unpleasant badgering of their father, not to mention her constant criticism of women not in her bridge or garden groups, may have been what kept the two girls from slipping into similar behaviors.

It also led them to make two decisions: one, they loved their mother—they just didn't trust her; two, they would each live with a man for at least a year before agreeing to marry him. Only Erin had held firm to that decision, however. Mallory, who married right out of college and without living with her fiancé, found herself divorced after six years.

It was her "summer of distress," as she called it, that led Mallory into a brief relationship with her father's cute but confusing neighbor. Though she knew at the time that she and Ray weren't destined to be long term lovers, she also recognized that Ray wasn't destined to be anyone's long-term lover. But he had helped her through a hard time, and she had considered him a close friend ever since.

———————

Ray watched Josh cast, then said, "I'm going to keep that rod today and replace the line. That's half your problem."

"But you'll let me pay you for that?" asked Josh, concerned.

"You just be good to my buddy here and we're fine," said Ray. "I want to give you some good lures, too," said Ray. "Especially this Big Dawg, which is great for casting around lily pads and weeds. Perfect for a beginner like you, the Big Dawg is easy to cast, to skip, and to let sink . . . just like so."

He raised his rod to demonstrate, saying as he cast, "Josh, you can't fish this guy wrong. So here's the deal: I'll get you new line, check your reel, and give you enough to set you up to catch one of the big girls. How does that sound?"

"Amazing. But how do I decide where and when to go fish for these . . . 'big girls'?"

"My rule of thumb is pretty darn simple: fish dark lakes like Loon Lake on clear days and clear lakes—and Spider Lake is a good example and not too far from here—on dark days.

Then, using that Big Dawg, cast along the outside of weed beds like the one we're drifting by right now.

"Mallory, why don't you put that phone down and pay attention to what I'm telling Josh," said Ray, "so you can take him out in your old man's boat later."

"I'm listening, I'm listening," said Mallory, annoyed to be caught on her phone.

Sure he had her attention, Ray said, "I'm going to send you two over to that sandbar over there." He pointed.

"Mallory knows where I mean. The water is deep on both sides, which is great for muskies, because smaller muskies like to run in a pack. They're predators and they love to hang out, watching for smaller fish they can ambush, which is what makes a sandbar the perfect place to find 'em.

"You just wait," said Ray, nudging Josh's shoulder. "Once you see that, once you have a lunker on the line—buddy, you'll be hooked." His enthusiasm was so catching that Josh grinned happily as he cast again.

"Oh, no," said Ray, grabbing the rod away from him, "you got a problem with this old reel, too. Tell you what, Josh, leave this rod with me and I've got a Garcia Ambassadeur Series 5000 I can give you. Just got myself a new 6500, so I don't mind giving up my old one.

"It'll make a difference—the handle won't snap out of your hand if you catch a big girl, plus it's easier on letting line out if a fish is running, especially if you're a beginner. . . ."

Ray was still talking when the shrill of an ambulance siren cut through the air.

# CHAPTER ELEVEN

"That siren sounds very close," said Ray, swinging the boat around toward the south shore of the lake. They could hear the siren moving along the road until flashing lights could be seen through the trees at a distance from where they were on the water.

For a few moments, Ray let the boat drift as he scanned the shoreline. "Sorry to interrupt the fishing," he said. "I want to be sure no one needs help. . . ."

The flashing lights continued, although the siren finally had been shut off. They could see figures moving out along a dock next to which was moored a pontoon.

"That's Kara's place, I think," said Ray.

"You don't mean Kara Kudelik?" asked Mallory. "We were in school together. She got a master's after college and teaches at Loon Lake High now."

"Yep, that's Kara," said Ray, slowing the boat as he got closer to the dock. "She recently bought that white house up on the hill that you pass on the way out to my place. Nice woman, always waves."

As their boat got closer, they could see three EMTs who appeared to be helping a person out of the water.

"Ooh, I hope whoever fell in is okay," said Mallory, wincing. "I really hope it isn't Kara. She's been a good friend for years. We used to get together for coffee when I was up visiting, but I haven't caught up with her in a while."

"Excuse me, Dick—" Ray cut the motor as he shouted so the EMT he had recognized could hear him. "You got what you need? Can I help in any way? Is everyone okay?"

The young EMT raised his arms in defeat. "Too late, Pradt. She's been in the water a while." Now Ray let the boat drift to within twenty feet of the dock. "We've got a call in to the police department—afraid we're gonna need the coroner to confirm the drowning."

"That would be Dad," said Mallory in a low voice. "I think he's home trying to get some sleep after helping Chief Ferris with that terrible murder-suicide yesterday. Think I should call him?"

"No," said Ray, "he'll hear from the chief if he hasn't already. Say, Dick, who did you say the drowning victim is?"

"I didn't and I'm not supposed to," said the EMT, "but you're a neighbor, aren't you? We need to reach next of kin ASAP. According to the neighbor who called 911, it's Kara Kudelik. Doesn't she have family nearby?"

"Yes," said Ray, "her parents live in Rhinelander. Father's name is Bernie—Bernard Kudelik. I think they still live up on Lake Shore Drive. . . ."

Before he could finish, the EMT had found the number on his cell phone and waved at Ray, "Found 'em, thanks," and turned to run toward the ambulance.

"Brother, way to ruin an afternoon," said Ray with a grim

set to his mouth as he turned the boat away from the dock. As the boat sped up, he shouted so Josh and Mallory could hear, "At least we're close to that sandbar I was talking about. Show you right where to go. . . ." In a couple minutes, he cut the motor to let the boat drift. "Look down, Josh. Even with this dark water, you can see the sandbar, right?"

Josh and Mallory peered over the gunwales to where he was pointing and nodded when they could see it.

"So, Josh, quite a few smaller muskies hang out here, waiting to ambush the panfish that love this spot. It's only when they get much bigger that the lunkers hunt alone in deeper holes or along weed beds.

"That makes fishing here a good exercise: you can practice doing your figure eights alongside the boat when you get a follow. If you're lucky enough to have one take your hook, you'll get a lesson in how to land a big fish. Remember, I might call 'em 'small,' but even the smaller girls are fighters. Plenty to learn from."

---

Osborne was pouring himself a late-morning cup of coffee when the kitchen phone rang. He picked up the remote, wondering who it could be. Lew, Ray, his daughters—people who knew him almost always called his cell these days.

"Paul." The voice on the phone was curt, tight.

"Yes?" The voice sounded familiar but Osborne couldn't place it.

"Bernie Kudelik here."

"Good morning, Bernie," said Osborne, walking toward his

front porch, coffee cup in hand and wondering if Bernie hadn't got the message he was retired and was calling with a dental emergency. Or maybe he just needed a referral.

"Just got a call from the sheriff's department that Pecore's in the hospital and you're deputy coroner for Loon Lake—"

"Yes, but—"

"You haven't heard?" Even as Bernie asked the question, Osborne's cell phone rang: it was the Loon Lake Police Department.

"They're calling me right now. Can I call you back?"

"No," the man's voice thundered. "No, goddammit. They're calling to tell you my daughter, Kara, is dead. Drowned they said. She didn't drown, Paul. I *know* she didn't drown."

"Okay, Bernie. Take it easy. I'm listening." Osborne switched into the tone of voice he had used when patients, usually hockey players, called semihysterical to announce one or more teeth had been knocked out and they were bleeding. . . .

"Kara . . ."—Bernie paused, and Osborne could hear him choke back sobs—"she told me she has been getting strange phone calls, threatening phone calls—Paul, she didn't drown. Some crazy person . . ." He couldn't finish. Osborne waited, unsure what to say. "I want an autopsy," said Bernie at last. "An autopsy, goddammit." He hung up.

Checking his phone Osborne could see he had had two calls from the Loon Lake Police. Has to be Lew, he thought as he hit CALL BACK.

"I'll put you through to Chief Ferris," said the dispatcher the moment she answered.

"Doc? Sorry, but we have another fatality for you to handle," said Lew. "Not far from your home—"

"Kara Kudelik?"

"Yes, the Fire Department called to say their EMTs were called out to rescue a drowning victim. They got there too late. They said they reached the family and told them you were acting coroner—"

"That's why I didn't answer your call. I just heard from Karen's father, Bernie Kudelik. He wants an autopsy, Lew."

"Tell him he has to pay for it," said Lew, interrupting. "They can cost ten grand or more. For heaven's sake, his daughter has *drowned*—he doesn't need an autopsy."

"That's not what he thinks. He said she has been receiving threatening calls."

"What kind of calls?"

"I didn't have time to ask. You kept calling me. But I'm on my way over right now. The EMT crew is waiting."

Lew was quiet, and he knew she was debating calling for an autopsy. If she did, her department and the town would have to pay. "I've already got the two Powers victims scheduled, guess I better add this one, too. You agree?"

"Given what Bernie said, yes. But if I see any reason not to, you will hear from me within the hour." He hesitated, there had been a tone in her voice that worried him. "Are you okay?"

"Just worried. So far Bruce and his team haven't a single lead on who might have killed the Powers couple."

"Suicide ruled out?"

"Yes, according to Bruce's investigator who's the expert on gunshot wounds. Neither died from a self-inflicted gunshot.

But no sign of the gun that they now know was used to fire the bullets that killed both the husband and wife."

"Okay, Lew. Just got in the car and heading over to Kara's place. Her home is only a third of a mile from here. Be back in touch shortly."

# CHAPTER TWELVE

A white Ford pickup was parked on the road beside the short drive up to Kara Kudelik's small frame house. An ambulance was blocking the drive, so Osborne parked behind the pickup, grabbed his black instrument bag and the clipboard holding the documents needed to initiate the death certificate. He started toward the ambulance.

"Paul," said a man running toward him from the front door of the small house. Osborne recognized Bernie Kudelik. "Wait, let me talk to you," Bernie insisted.

"Bernie, I passed your concern on to Chief Ferris. She's on her way and she's the person you need to talk to. As deputy coroner all I do is confirm—"

"I know all that," said Bernie with an impatient wave of his arms. "I'm a retired criminal defense lawyer. But our daughters grew up together, went to high school together, and they've stayed in touch over the years." On seeing that Osborne had stopped to listen, Bernie relaxed and spoke more slowly.

"Here's the thing, Paul. Kara and Mallory used to have coffee together. I'm wondering if maybe Kara ever said anything to her about these calls she was getting. See, the calls started about a month ago, right after Karen started seeing someone. . . ."

"'Someone'?" asked Osborne. "Who is the 'someone'? And, Bernie, Mallory hasn't seen Kara in quite a while. I don't think she would have heard anything, but I will ask just in case. Mallory is up visiting now. But do you know who this 'someone' is?"

"See, that's what she wouldn't tell me." Bernie lowered his voice. "I'm pretty sure she was seeing some guy going through a divorce."

"A married man."

"Right. I don't know why," said Bernie, his eyes clouded with sorrow, "and maybe it was my fault. Her mother divorced me years ago, and she was right. I was stupid; I played around a few too many times. And Kara? She just seemed to latch on to the bad boys. You know what I mean?"

Osborne nodded in understanding though he didn't understand. Not really. He never had. He had watched men he knew to be in marriages much more pleasant than his own (at least that's how they seemed to him) who were inveterate flirts. Sometimes worse, badgering women if they didn't appear to appreciate the attention. Just watching the men's behavior made him uncomfortable, and later he would encourage his daughters to avoid men like that.

"You said she was getting threatening calls," said Osborne. "From a man or a woman? Maybe someone's wife?"

"She never told me exactly. I think she was so frightened she couldn't bring herself to repeat them—they were so ugly. She was so shaken by a call she got last week that she asked me for help tracing it. I called a retired detective who used to do insurance investigations for our law firm, but all he could find was that it came from a prepaid cell phone, so no luck."

Osborne paused, then asked, "Bernie, do you know if Kara was friends with John and Margo Powers?"

"Who? Not that I know of. Never heard the names. If she was, she never mentioned it. Why?"

"Just wondering. Please forget I asked. Bernie, Chief Ferris is going to hope you can tell her more."

"I'll do my best," he choked out as tears rolled down his cheeks. "How could my daughter drown? She was captain of her college swim team."

Minutes later, after viewing Kara Kudelik's body and confirming her death, Osborne felt a tap on his shoulder. He turned to see Don Flatley, a veteran on the EMT team with whom he had worked often when substituting for an "ailing" Pecore.

"Doc," said Don, beckoning him over to one side of the ambulance inside which Kara's body was resting on a gurney before being transported to the morgue at St. Mary's Hospital, "you know I'm no expert—certainly no MD—but I've seen a lot of dead people, y'know."

While Don's approach sounded a little macabre, Osborne found his blithe manner refreshing. "They say we rescue folks," said Don, "and half the time we do. Bike accidents, car crashes, and . . . drownings. But just as often we're here just to put words to the hard thing. When someone drowns, I've seen enough I know the signs."

"I'm sure you do, but—"

"I just want to say this may not be an accident, Doc. Can you do an autopsy?"

"Well, not me, certainly," said Osborne. "I'm a retired dentist, and as deputy coroner all I do is confirm that the party is deceased."

"Right. I knew that," said Don. "But you can make sure there's an autopsy, right?"

"Chief Ferris makes that decision. She's on her way out here now."

"Oh, good, I'll talk to her," said Don. He turned to walk away, then stopped. "I knew Kara. She taught both my kids. A very nice woman."

"Don," said Osborne, "are you telling me you saw something?"

"All I'm saying is she did not drown. I just don't see it. But, Doc, like I said, I'm no expert."

"Just a damn good EMT," said Osborne. As he started to walk away, a familiar police cruiser drove past the crowded driveway. "Don, there's Chief Ferris now. Please tell her what you just told me."

# CHAPTER THIRTEEN

On Monday morning Lew was up by 5:00 a.m. with plans to be in her office by six. She was hoping to get a jump on the paperwork piling up, not to mention alerting the mayor that she would be adding to the town budget with another ten-thousand-dollar autopsy.

She could hear him already, the razzbonya responsible for appointing his boozing brother-in-law, Ed Pecore, to the position of Loon Lake coroner: "Honestly, Lewellyn, it's just another drowning. Don Flatley is an idiot—you know that. I don't care if he is an experienced EMT."

What her esteemed mayor did care about, Lew knew, was that Don Flatley had been married to his daughter for a tumultuous three years. Their divorce had left the mayor and his wife annually lobbying for Don's dismissal from the EMT team, but they were always stymied. Loon Lake's fire chief, Don's cousin, refused to let that happen and for good reason: "He's well trained, experienced, and politics be damned."

"Never say family connections don't work both ways," Lew would say, grinning as she repeated his words to Osborne every January. She was grinning to herself again as she walked out onto her dock, coffee cup in hand, when a figure standing on the neighbors' dock five hundred yards away waved at her and called, "Good morning, can I walk over and talk to you?"

Lew didn't recognize the woman shouting at her across the water, but she waved back anyway. Five minutes later she could hear someone scrambling through the trees and brush crowding the shoreline.

"Sorry to interrupt your morning, but I know you leave early," said a brisk female voice. "Good to meet you, Chief Ferris. I'm Diane Armeo, and I'll be directing the team working on the computer project in your neighbors' barn. Heard a lot about you from my FBI colleagues." She stepped forward with a hand out to shake Lew's.

Lew could hear authority in her voice and see a no-nonsense attitude in her eyes. She felt comfortable right away with the woman. "And you're still talking to me?" asked Lew, raising her coffee cup in surrender.

"Your fly-fishing expertise is what I'm interested in," said Diane. "I've wanted to find the time to learn to fly fish for years. Been traveling too much and working in all the wrong places." She smiled as she said, "So here I am in the middle of nowhere and what do you know but there's a fly-fishing guru right next door to my office."

"I wouldn't go that far," said Lew, deciding not to comment on the reference to a nearby office. "More coffee?" They headed inside.

"Sure, I'd love one more cup. Yeah, I grew up in New Jersey and my parents were not very outdoorsy. I was a renegade, went to summer camp up in Maine, went to college in New Hampshire—I fell in love with the outdoors. Done a lot of camping, hiking, scuba diving, and, of course, survival training, but not much fishing, though I love being around water—on it, in it—you name it."

"That's right, you're retired from the NSA," said Lew. "That must have been quite a career."

Diane's face tightened, a shadow clouding her eyes for an instant before she said, "You'll understand if I don't discuss my work?"

"Sorry," said Lew, with a shrug. "I should know better."

Diane smiled, stood up from the kitchen table where they had been sitting, and poured herself another cup of coffee. She checked her watch. "What time do you need to leave? I don't want to keep you, Chief."

"Why don't we do this," said Lew. "You call me Lew, and I'll call you Diane, and we'll go fishing. And no shop talk—yours or mine."

"That works for me . . . Lew." As Diane spoke, sunlight brightened the kitchen and Lew felt good.

"So here's my problem," said Lew. "I've got a colleague leaning on me for some help with his casting. Actually I have two guys I work with who need help. One I can fish with any-time because, well, he lives in town, but Bruce—you'll meet Bruce if we go this week—is up from Wausau, which is an hour away. If I agree to coach him in the trout stream, he'll cut me a deal on investigative work he's doing for my depart-ment and right now, budget-wise, that is very helpful."

"I get that," said Diane, "so I should tag along with you and two guys?"

"If you want a lesson sooner rather than later. I'll instruct them not to ask questions."

"And they'll understand?"

"They know," said Lew. "You'll enjoy meeting them, too. Good guys."

"Not too expert that I'm going to frustrate them 'cause I'm such a beginner?"

"Don't worry about that. They've got a lot to learn, those two, but they do catch fish, so they keep working at it."

"Wonderful," said Diane, slapping the table and heading for the door. "When you're ready, you'll find me next door or at that Loon Lake Motel in town."

"How long will you be here?" asked Lew.

"Long enough that I'm looking for a cottage to rent, so let me know if you have a suggestion." And with that she was out the door.

---

It was almost seven thirty when Lew got to her office, only to discover Bruce and his laptop computer had taken over half the room. The armchairs and small coffee table, which she liked to use for informal meetings, were hidden under unruly stacks of photos and documents. "Should I move out?" asked Lew, pausing to study the mess.

"The light in here is much better than your conference room," said Bruce, sounding like he had had too much coffee. He may have. A quick glance at her coffeemaker in the far corner showed it less than half full.

Bruce ignored her teasing as he held up one of Ray's black-and-white five-by-tens and studied it. "Funny, how a good print shows up so well compared to the digital version," he said as he turned his laptop's screen so she could see what he meant.

"No breakthrough yet on the Powers murders, I'm afraid. Just got off the phone with that lawyer of theirs. Thought you'd like to know that they're hitting dead ends down south, too. I set up a conference call for everyone late this morning. But I do have good news . . . well, good news for us, not for anyone else."

"Before you tell me," said Lew, "I need to say I sure hope you take better care organizing your trout flies than what I'm seeing thrown across that coffee table."

Bruce gave her a broad smile, his dark, bushy eyebrows dancing as he said, "My wife complains I should take such good care with my underwear drawer as I do with my fishing gear. But, Chief," he said, tipping his chair back to gloat, "you're going to be p-u-u-l-e-n-t-y surprised with what one of my team discovered early this morning on your Kudelik murder case. . . ."

"The autopsy is complete already?" Lew was surprised.

"No, the pathologist has scheduled that for this afternoon, but he did a cursory exam when the ambulance arrived late last night and he said that drowning as a cause of death was highly suspect."

Lew opened her mouth to speak but Bruce interrupted before she could, saying, "I have two investigators working out at the house right now. They drove up from Wausau late last night." Again the eyebrows flipped up and down as Bruce made her wait a maddening moment.

"So they get to the woman's house this morning, walk into her kitchen, and find a cast-iron frying pan sitting cat-awampus on the stove—a frying pan that has hairs stuck to the bottom. Not short little hairs like something on your apron or your shirt but long, dark brown hairs, which may match the victim's hair.

"Now the question is, how does that happen?" He stared at Lew.

She returned the stare. "Are there fingerprints on the frying pan handle?"

"I doubt it, though possibly the victim's, but I imagine that if that pan turns out to be the murder weapon, you can be sure the perpetrator wouldn't be so stupid as to leave fingerprints all over the place. But they did leave something else . . . we hope. Remember, the victim was found in the water near her dock. . . ."

"Correct," said Lew and waited patiently.

This was why she never hesitated to spend time teaching Bruce whatever he needed to learn in the trout stream: he was terrific to work with, a smart guy whose forensic talents had a way of making her look good.

"Well, Miss Kudelik had conveniently watered some new grass she had planted early yesterday morning. As a result, we have footprints going down to the dock area *and* we have Miss Kudelik's shoes—all twenty-one pairs. We will be checking to see which, if any, of her shoes match those footprints.

"Our theory is simple: our victim did not walk herself down to the dock and into the water. Someone made that happen, someone who had to walk down there carrying an extra hundred-plus pounds."

Bruce closed his eyes and tightened his lips. "You know, if only we had that kind of luck at the Powers place. Darn."

"How many of the Wausau Crime Lab people are working up here right now, Bruce?" asked Lew, realizing that two crime scenes might pose a problem for the crime lab staff. After all, Wausau had its problems, plus they helped out three other towns.

"Let me put it this way, Chief, if you have any more unexplained deaths up here, I'll have to call in backup from Madison or Green Bay. Right now, we've booked every free room they had at the Loon Lake Motel. Some woman from the East Coast got the last one yesterday morning."

"I know who that is," said Lew, "you'll meet her shortly. I think you'll be intrigued, Bruce."

"Just so she's not a yoga teacher—my wife keeps bugging me to sign up for yoga classes."

"She is not a yoga teacher. She's retired from the NSA."

Bruce's eyebrows appeared to hit his hairline.

# CHAPTER FOURTEEN

"W-h-a-a—?"

The astonishment on Bruce's face pleased Lew. It wasn't often she had the chance to surprise him.

"We've had so much going on I haven't had a chance to tell you that my next-door neighbors' old PC computer was taken over by hackers from outside the country who have been trying to hack into major companies, maybe even the U.S. government," said Lew. "A group of tech experts have been brought in to investigate the hackers involved, which is how I met Diane Armeo.

"She runs a cybersecurity firm that works to detect and block security breaches." After a dramatic pause, knowing what she was about to say would intrigue Bruce no end, Lew said, "Diane was formerly with the NSA but, Bruce, her agency work is something she wants kept confidential. In other words, *you cannot ask her about that*." Lew gave him a hard look.

He got the message. "I know, I know," he said, "my brother, Ben, works cybersecurity for a start-up down in Madison that's responsible for banks and a network of hospitals. That is one challenging field. Ben said the technology changes daily.

"Gosh, Chief," said Bruce with such enthusiasm that Lew could see she'd hit on one of his favorite subjects (aside from fly-fishing, that is), "one of their client banks—a big one—got hit by hackers over three hundred thousand times. And that's just *one* bank. Now he said they don't call what they do 'security' so much as 'threat intelligence.' And you're saying that's what this woman is working on?"

"Bruce, all I know is she's in charge of this particular cybersecurity operation—and that is all I know. Maybe she's working for the Feds, maybe for the Rhinelander Public Library. I haven't the faintest idea for whom she's doing the work. All I do know is that it's none of my business—or yours."

"Hackers from another country going after U.S. companies from some outdated computer they found out here in the boonies?" Bruce was dubious. "Give me a break, and hey, if it's so top secret, Chief, how did you find out about it?"

Hoping to shut him up, Lew gave him the dim eye. Then she relented. She was darn curious herself.

"Strictly by accident," she said, lightening up. "The other morning Doc and I were trying to find where our grandchildren had disappeared to. After searching all around my place and no sign of the little stinkers, I decided they must have run next door to play with my neighbors' dogs.

"When we got there, I found the cybersecurity guys who work for the state parked in my neighbors' driveway. I knew the guy in charge and he recognized me right away—we met last month at a conference in Green Bay. He told me his people had tracked a group of hackers to this old, dusty computer in my neighbors' barn—a PC they use for billing their sawmill customers.

"Turns out experts have discovered eight or nine major hacking sites like this across the country—computers in remote locations hijacked to be used as conduits, pipelines that allow them to access the networks and data belonging to businesses of all types—banks, health care, law firms, tech companies, retailers. The off-the-grid locations make them easy to hide, hard to find."

"Sounds like just the work my brother does. I tell you, Chief, makes me feel old-fashioned. I'll bet anything your new pal is setting up to watch the sons of bitches. Watch 'em and stop 'em. That's what Ben does."

"All I know for sure," said Lew, "is that while she's up here in the northwoods, she wants to learn how to fly fish. So if I bring her along with us later this week, can I count on you not to ask too many questions?"

Lew waited. Bruce furrowed his brow.

"So, like, this is a promise? The lesson, I mean?" he asked.

"Of course. But we have two cases to work on. I don't know when we can possibly—"

"Wednesday." Bruce leaped up from his chair. "Wednesday unless we have bad weather. I got the Powers crime scene covered: procedures in place, log under way, integrity of the site is well established. . . ."

"But we may have two," said Lew. "This is a lot of work for a small number of people."

"You promise me Wednesday afternoon and I'll see we get it done."

After attaching his used Garcia Ambassadeur reel to Josh's muskie rod, Ray was in the midst of putting new line on it when his cell phone sent Wanda Jackson's "Let's Have a Party" bouncing off the walls of his kitchen. He'd forgotten he'd put the song on his ringtone late the day before in an effort to impress the cute new clerk at the Happy Hookers bait shop.

"Ray Pradt, you lovely man?" His heart sank at the sound of Judith Kerr's voice. Darn, he had hoped she wouldn't call. "Are we on for later this afternoon? I can't wait, honeybun."

Honeybun yourself, he thought as he pulled his calendar across the table, hoping he had a doctor visit scheduled. Maybe even a colonoscopy, but no such luck. He was about to agree to a time for her to show up at his place, when another call dinged his phone: CHIEF FERRIS. "Judith, let me call you back in five," he said, "got a call I have to take."

"No problemo, sweetie," she said and clicked off.

"Ray, this is not a good day," said Lew after he had hit the button to accept her call. "Kara Kudelik—"

"I know," said Ray, interrupting, "she drowned yesterday, poor woman. Why do you need me, Chief?"

"Kara did not drown. We just got an autopsy report stating she died of blunt force trauma. Someone bludgeoned her to death in her kitchen with a heavy cast-iron skillet.

"Bruce has two of his people out at her home right now, but you live so close that we're hoping we can get you over there to shoot the crime scene, especially since we're a day late already. Would that be a problem? I know you may have a guiding client—"

"No, no," said Ray, "happy to do it."

"Thank goodness. I'm putting Bruce on to tell you exactly what they need, as they want more outdoor shots than usual."

After the instructions from Bruce, Ray called Judith to cancel her lesson. They rescheduled for Tuesday, with Ray silently praying for thunderstorms that afternoon.

When he was off the phone from Judith, he sat quiet for a long time, saddened by the news about Kara. Her drowning had been bad enough, as she'd been a friend. More than a friend, really. Kara was one of his "girls"—one of the half dozen single women of varied ages whom he liked to surprise with a Friday afternoon gift of bluegills: fresh caught, filleted, and ready for the skillet.

Now two of his favorite women were missing: first was old and crotchety but wonderfully acerbic Lillian Curran and now graceful, kind Kara. He decided to drop by Lillian's place on the way to photograph Kara's home and kitchen, a kitchen once comfortable and welcoming—now fraught with images so disturbing Ray realized this was one assignment he might grow to hate.

---

It wasn't until Lew had the assurance Ray could step in and handle the photography at the Kudelik site that she realized how stressed she had been feeling. Bruce's presence in her office didn't help. He kept interrupting her concentration with calls he had to make; then there was the thumping of his fingers on the keys of his laptop. She loved the guy but enough was enough. She decided to take a quick stroll around the courthouse.

The late June morning was full of summer promise: the weigela shrubs encircling the courthouse lawn were tipped with pale pink blossoms that infused the air. Lew loved the soft fragrance, which reminded her of her childhood and a distant memory of a mother who had walked her down a path once upon a time that smelled just like this. She inhaled deeply and let her thoughts wander.

My life is so busy, she was thinking when she got a glimpse of a television crew set up on the north side of the building. The two men who were being interviewed were executives from John Powers's company. Pausing so as not to catch the attention of the TV crew, she listened as the men stated there had been no break in the case: "We're still scrambling to figure out how this could possibly have happened," said one.

Lew walked on. Regret lingered over how little time she'd had to spend with Suzanne and Becky, though she knew her daughter understood. And poor Doc. Twice she had turned down invitations to spend the night at his place. Usually, when she declined an offer from him, she would encourage him to stay over at her farmhouse, but she had been too tired for that, too.

She reached for her cell phone and hit his number. "Hey, stranger," said Doc, "you've caught me down on the dock searching for Cody's nightcrawlers. Kid is distraught thinking the eagle got 'em." His voice, familiar and sounding pleased to hear from her, settled her heart.

"And the answer is . . . ?" Lew waited, anticipating news

of an eagle that had recently enjoyed the breakfast of champions.

"Ha—found them. They're right here under his seat in the boat. Good thing Cody has a responsible grandfather. How's your day going?"

"Better. Ray is shooting the Kudelik place for Bruce, but I've got reams of paperwork on my desk plus I need to catch up with Todd and Roger."

"Let me know if Roger met with those kids who moved the buoys, will you, please? I'd like to check with the two fellas who take care of buoys for our lake association and make sure they are aware of what the kids were up to. I'm sure they are, but just in case.

"Oh, and if you're not too busy this evening, I have some venison I'm planning to—"

"Just tell me what time you're serving, Chef Osborne, and I'll be there. With a frozen wild blueberry pie from my freezer if that doesn't clash with your menu?"

"I'd say we have a deal," said Osborne.

"Oh, and, Doc, I'm taking Bruce and a new friend, Diane, fly-fishing Wednesday afternoon. Care to join us?"

"Now, Lewellyn," said Osborne, "what did I tell you when we first met?"

"Um, refresh my memory."

"Why does a man practice dentistry? So he can afford to fish." He smiled. "Invitation accepted."

# CHAPTER FIFTEEN

Ray gunned the boat across the lake to a spot where his clients could be sure to catch something, even it if was only a crappie. The goal this late afternoon was to put happiness on their faces, a fish or two on their stringer—and get rid of them as fast as possible. Seldom had he been forced to fish with two less pleasant people.

"Oh, Bill-y," chortled Judith when Kimble accidentally swung his rod around so the wet lure slapped her shoulder. She responded with a lingering squeeze of her friend's shoulder.

Please, God, spare me, thought Ray as he did his professional best to be sure Judith had her rod ready for action. She had a bad habit of touching him every time he got close, so he kept a good arm's length away. He even managed to get her to her feet and casting without making physical contact.

She had lied, of course: she was no novice when it came to fishing. He could tell the woman had held a spinning rod before. And cast. And likely caught plenty of fish, maybe even tarpon and a whale. Who knew?

But, hey, he was beginning to understand what was happening here. He should have known from the get-go, but he was so irritated by Judith's flirtatious manner that it took him a while to realize she was like that around men—all men, any man, she was nuts.

Today her attention was all on Kimble, and that razz-bonya didn't seem to mind in the least. Ray wasn't surprised. Was it his most recent girlfriend, Dawn, who had said what he'd heard many times before? She'd commented after watching Kimble in action at the Birchwood Bar: "That guy is unreal—talk about 'playing around'—he gives new meaning to the phrase. You have to wonder where he finds the energy."

Well, thought Ray, somebody's got a little too much energy today. Let's hope a fish comes by to break up this cozy little scene.

"How 'bout one more hour, folks?" He had had the two out in the boat since shortly after lunch.

"Sure," said Bill, turning a grinning face toward Ray. One thing Ray had noticed was that as much as Judith hovered over Bill, he didn't reach out to touch her very often. On the other hand, he had agreed to come fishing, so he must have known what she had in mind when he got her invitation.

Maybe, thought Ray, he knew better than to be too demonstrative around me, since he runs into me around town. Playing it cool so I won't think he's having an affair with this one. Well, bud, good luck. Pretty obvious what's going on here, and it has little to do with hooking a walleye. More like "hooking up."

"So, yes, I traveled internationally all the time," Judith was bragging to Bill as Ray listened with half an ear. "I cannot tell you what I was doing during my travels because that is not allowed when you work for the NSA. All I can say is I've seen a lot of the world, trust me." Then she nudged him in the shoulder, giggled, and let her Big Dawg lure fly.

"Does your job mean you have to carry a gun?" asked Bill, sounding impressed. "Or did I ask you that already?"

Ray had already deduced that they had connected during their high school reunion over Memorial Day, and he assumed it had likely been a well-lubricated event. So much so that it was no surprise that Bill might not remember their conversation. When it came to Wisconsin's state sport—beer drinking—Bill Kimble was a high scorer. No short hitter he.

And Judith, happy for the opportunity to remind him how special she was, said, "You did ask and I told you questions about my work are off-limits. Sorry, Billy. That's the price I pay for working at a very, very high level in our federal government.

"Hey, I got a bite!" Judith jumped to her feet, rocking the boat so much that Ray and Bill grabbed gunwales with both hands. "Oh, golly, Ray, can you help me please?"

She threw a look of helplessness in Ray's direction. He knew she was faking it: you don't cast, reel, and set a hook so neatly by accident. But he moved to take the rod from her hands while, squealing with excitement, she leaned over to hold tight to Bill.

The soft trill of a cell phone could be heard as Ray lifted the smallmouth bass toward the net he was holding in his left hand. Bill patted his shirt pockets before standing to pull his phone from his pants pocket.

"Hi, Evie, what's up? I told you I'm out fishing and not to call—"

Ray could hear a woman's voice high and shrill, sounding frantic.

"Okay, okay, I'll be home in an hour. Put the damn dogs in the kennel, Evie. They're going nuts over a squirrel is all. Will you settle down, please? I'll be there shortly . . . oh, well, that bad? I see . . . wow . . . you're sure about that . . . okay, go to the vet's, then. I'll meet you there—bye."

Off the phone, Bill looked at Ray and Judith. "Evie was walking our two dogs and they tried to climb over a barbed wire fence a neighbor just put up on our property line. Goofy guy thinks he owns five feet more than our deed shows—the jerk. Dogs tried to jump it and they're bleeding all over the place, she said. She's taking 'em to the vet and I've got to meet her there.

"Sorry, Judith," he said, patting her on the knee. "Ray, do you mind taking us in? I better get going."

"Happy to do it," said Ray. "Your dogs could be pretty torn up. Barbed wire is evil. Are you sure rigging wire like that is legal?"

"We'll find out." Bill had a grim look on his face.

---

The midafternoon sun pouring into her office through the tall, wide windows facing southwest had the effect of making Lew ever so slightly drowsy and making her wish she could sneak in a ten-minute nap. The sudden ring of her desk phone startled her.

"Chief Ferris? This is Peter Kelly, one of the lawyers trying to help the authorities down here in the Chicago area with some potential leads on the Powers murders. I may have a breakthrough in the case but I want to talk to you first if you've got the time."

Lew straightened up. What was that about a nap?

# CHAPTER SIXTEEN

t least, I think it's a breakthrough, but I need your help."

"Sure, go right ahead," said Lew, pushing the report she'd been reading aside and reaching for her notepad.

"This may sound nutty, but my wife is, I mean *was*, friends with Margo Powers. Though they were not the closest of friends, they ran in the same social circle—lunch together, work out together, some 'girls' trip' travels together. You must know what I mean."

"I do," said Lew. "I know lots of women like that."

"She told me something I was not aware of. She said that all the women who knew Margo knew that she and John were having problems. Seems Margo didn't hesitate to share with 'the girls' that she was enjoying an affair with someone up north where you are, Chief.

"I have no idea who that is, but my wife said that she knew Margo was seeing a shrink down here, excuse me, I should say a psychiatrist. I know who that is." His voice took on a wry tone as he said, "Seems all the women married to men I know see the same shrink, I mean doctor, I mean . . ."

"It's okay, I got it," said Lew. "Have you talked to that person? They may shed some light on this, though I'm sure there is doctor-patient privilege that we need to be mindful of."

"That's exactly why I called you. You're a woman, you may have better luck than me calling cold. And, who knows, this may be a crazy idea of mine, but . . ."

"But worth checking out," said Lew. "Mr. Kelly—"

"The name is Peter."

"Okay, Peter."

"And I was thinking we might do a conference call if you're okay with that?"

"Of course, so long as we fully inform the doctor of the reason for our call and that I'll be taping the call."

"Sure . . ."

"Were you thinking of doing this right now?"

"Yes. I called Dr. Hardy's office, and she's available shortly for about fifteen minutes."

"Let me call you right back," said Lew. "I have a deputy whom I would like to have on the call, too. He's very experienced in this kind of questioning."

"Fine," said Peter, and he gave her the conference call number to call in on.

Off the phone with Peter Kelly, Lew called Osborne's cell phone and held her breath, hoping he would answer.

---

She had learned early in their time working together that Osborne was an excellent listener. While she listened for the facts—for the answers to her questions—Osborne knew how to look and listen for what lay hidden behind the obvious.

"It's a skill I learned early in my dental practice," he once told her. "One patient may be complaining of pain when what they really need is attention, someone to listen to them. Another may come into my office for an annual exam and complain that allergies are causing certain symptoms while I can see it's the use of controlled substances that's the source of their problem.

"How do I let that patient know that I know the true nature of their problem? It's delicate, but I do my best to encourage them to get the kind of help they really need."

He was especially attuned to people, most often women, insisting they had problems with their bite or another cosmetic whitening when all they really needed was to be cared for in a thoughtful, kind way by their good-looking dentist. A dentist whose expert and honest opinion could save them a lot of money.

---

"So, Doc," said Lew after giving him a brief description of Peter Kelly's plan to talk with Margo Powers's psychiatrist. "I know this will be a difficult conversation and I doubt the psychiatrist will be in a position to say much, but I would appreciate your take on whatever is discussed. Do you have time if we do this right now?"

"Yes," said Osborne, "on the condition we can discuss it further over dinner at my place this evening." He crossed his fingers, hoping she would agree to dinner again even if it meant spending two nights in a row at his place (which was just how he liked it).

"Agreed," said Lew with a chuckle of relief.

Minutes later they were in conversation with Peter Kelly and Dr. Eleanor Hardy.

"I see," said Dr. Hardy after Peter had described the murder scene and the early leads being pursued by the Wausau Crime Lab, the Loon Lake Police, and the authorities in Evanston and Chicago, "but I can't be of much help, I'm afraid. For one thing, my professional responsibility to my patient means that whatever she has told me must remain confidential.

"What I can say is that nothing we discussed could ever have led to such a terrible crime. Nothing."

"Dr. Hardy," said Osborne after introducing himself and mentioning his dental experience as well as his forensic expertise, "what we are looking for is any information that you might have that might have put your patient at risk."

"I know that," said Dr. Hardy, "and I can't think of anything or any person. I'm sorry. Margo Powers was a woman working hard to resolve emotional issues—her own issues. She didn't talk about other people."

"Are you free to tell us if she was having an affair with someone living up in this area?" asked Lew.

"No. I am not free to tell you that. To do so would imply that somewhere there is a woman married to a man involved in an extramarital affair, and that could lead to people suspecting the wife of murdering the woman her husband is seeing. Do you see what you're asking me to say?"

She was right. Everyone on the call was silent for a long moment.

Dr. Hardy spoke again. "If it helps—and it won't—Margo never mentioned names during our sessions. I understand what you are trying to do and I know their family needs a resolution to this tragedy. Have you considered talking to Margo's close friends? And by that I mean her woman friends. I suggest you give that some thought."

"Dr. Hardy, I apologize before I ask you this question," said Osborne. "You have said that Margo never mentioned other people. But she had to have found you somehow. Do you know who recommended you as a psychiatrist?"

"One moment, Dr. Osborne," said Dr. Hardy, "let me check my file, as I do like to know how patients find me and I see no reason not to share that information. Hold for a minute . . . okay, here it is: I was recommended to Margo Powers by Robin Schumacher.

"Mr. Kelly, if your wife was a friend of Margo's, very likely she knows Robin, too. Sorry I can't be more help, everyone."

When Dr. Hardy had hung up from the call, Osborne said, "That was very helpful. And I'm sure the good Dr. Hardy knows it was, too. Peter, are you familiar with Robin Schumacher?"

"Oh, yes, she's another one of my wife's friends, though they aren't as close as Margo and Robin have been. I told Chief Ferris that all these women who know one another see the same shrink. Guess who knows more about our lives than we do," he said with a wry laugh. "Though I don't know her well, only from social gatherings, Robin has also struck me as a sensible, good person. She's an athlete."

Osborne found that remark amusing, as if being athletic made someone a good person.

"Should we do the same? The three of us talk with her together? I'm sure my wife will know how to reach Robin."

"I think it would be wise for the three of us to talk to her," said Lew. "Doc, okay with you?"

"Yes. This could be a dead end but worth a try. At least now we know someone local to Loon Lake or nearby was also involved with the Powers family."

"I wonder if John knew of Margo's affair?" asked Peter. "What if he did and was putting pressure on the guy?"

"Not only that," said Lew, "if Margo were to be divorced, I'm sure she would have ended up a very rich woman. Hate to say it, but Loon Lake has its share of nogoodniks who might take advantage of that."

"Hey," said Peter, "don't castigate Loon Lake—guys like that are everywhere."

# CHAPTER SEVENTEEN

After a quick check with his wife while Osborne and Lew remained on hold, Peter had the cell phone number for Robin Schumacher.

"I doubt we'll reach her right now," said Peter. "Why don't I leave a voice mail and ask her to return my call, after which we can work out a time for a conference call with all four of us? But stay on the line here in case she does answer. Okay?"

"Sounds fine to me," said Lew, and Osborne agreed. Peter placed the call and they waited.

"Robin is on the line," said Peter a moment later. "I reached her at home, and she is willing to talk to us. Ready?" And with that Lew and Osborne found themselves back on a conference call.

"Mrs. Schumacher," said Lew after introductions had been made, "how long have you known Margo Powers?"

"Since college," said a strong female voice, "and I'm still reeling from this news. She was a dear friend in spite of being a little ditsy sometimes. I just don't understand how this happened.

"But to answer your question I would say Margo and I have been friends for almost twenty years. Our husbands were college roommates, which is how we met. And call me Robin, please. 'Mrs. Schmacher' makes me sound like my mother-in-law." She gave a weak laugh, as though embarrassed to find anything humorous in the moment.

"Certainly," said Osborne, "and what kind of work do you do?" Osborne was surprised to find himself asking the question. Later he would tell Lew it was the tone of authority in the woman's voice that made him wonder what she did. Subtle though it might be, he had noticed over the years that people—men or women—who worked with others, who managed others, had a way of speaking with an air of confidence.

"I'm a commodities trader. You caught me at home today because one of my kids has the chicken pox, so no school, no day care. I'm just hoping I don't get it." Again the embarrassed laugh. "Not really, I had it as a kid. But back to Margo. Do you have any idea who might have done this?"

"That's why we're talking to you," said Peter. "My wife and I were thinking about Margo and how she was going up north alone a lot lately, so we thought maybe one of her close friends might know if there's some person or some people Chief Ferris and Dr. Osborne should be looking at more closely, maybe someone living up around their summer home.

"Investigators are looking into John's business activities and we know he was enmeshed in some messy lawsuits, but nothing has surfaced on that front. At least not yet. So I'm checking with friends of Margo's to see if she said anything recently—like if someone up north was bothering her—that sort of thing."

The conference line was quiet for a long moment.

"There is something," said Robin at last, "and I don't know

if I should be telling you this. . . . Margo has been having issues for the last year or so."

"Issues?" asked Lew. "Is she involved in lawsuits, too?"

"No, no, nothing like that. Emotional stuff. See, John's business has always been *kind of* successful, but two years ago, it really took off. He bought a couple small start-ups that did phenomenally well.

"A large part of that is John himself: he micromanages, and that means he has to be there on-site. John has a private plane, and he travels all the time. They never had kids, and Margo has never worked, so she's home twiddling her thumbs. Well, not really. I guess you know she was seeing a psychiatrist, right?"

"Yes," said Osborne, "but we don't know why exactly."

"I'll tell you why exactly," said Robin, her voice rising, "because she was fooling around with other men and someone was bound to tell her husband."

"Like you?" Osborne asked.

Again the silence. "Maybe . . . but I didn't want to for one reason. John is a dear friend of ours and I worried that he would be devastated. I didn't tell him, but I told Margo in no uncertain terms that she needed to get help or I *would* tell him."

Robin sighed. "I thought if she saw a good therapist who could help her get a better perspective on life, she would settle down. Let me explain something about Margo," said Robin, "but first, Chief Ferris, did you ever meet her?"

"No, but Dr. Osborne here did."

"Okay, Dr. Osborne, what did you think of her?"

"It was three years ago that I saw her for a tooth that

needed a crown," said Osborne, "shortly before I retired. She struck me as a nice person and a very pretty woman. Exceptionally pretty."

"Right," said Robin, "very pretty and quite used to being adored. To put it bluntly, my friend was needy; she needed attention, constant attention. And guess who wasn't around to . . ."

"Her husband."

"You got it. I believe I'm her only friend who told her straight-out to get help or she was going to ruin her marriage if not her life. I'm the reason why she was seeing Dr. Hardy."

"That doesn't answer our question about someone up north," said Lew. "Are you implying she might have been having an affair with someone up here?"

"I know she was," said Robin. "I was there when it started.

"Margo had invited me and several other women friends up for a weekend of kayaking. It was supposed to be a nice day, but when we got out in the middle of the lake, the wind came up and Margo's kayak capsized. It was crazy. We were all around her, struggling like hell to get her back into the kayak, which was not going to happen, when a pontoon with two fishermen showed up offering to help us.

"They pulled Margo on board the pontoon and one guy took off his shirt to keep her warm. They headed for shore and the boat landing, and we met up with them at a bar that was right next to the boat landing. One of the fishermen was this tall, handsome dude with the kind of smile that melts women—the whole package, y'know.

"I could see he was infatuated with this gorgeous mermaid he'd rescued, and Margo encouraged him as only Margo could. She might have been hosting the five of us girls but you'd never know it."

"You think she saw this man again?"

"I know she did—up until two weeks ago. Then she cut it off."

"She ended the affair?"

"Yes. Not because of Dr. Hardy, unfortunately, but because as she got to know him better, she didn't care for his behavior. He was a heavy drinker. I know he passed out at her place once right when John was flying in and she was frantic trying to get him out of the house before John got there. Oh, and one more item. She had started fooling around with someone down here, too.

"You know what I hate about telling you all this? I'm making Margo sound horrible when all she was—was a very lonely person. Her affairs weren't all her fault. John had something to do with that, too."

"Tell us more about the man who rescued her and—"

"He's a fisherman."

Lew snorted. "*That* does not help much, sorry. What does he look like?"

"Quite tall and well built like maybe he used to play football. Dark hair, wide face, very pleasant manner. Oh, and he's married."

"Did Margo know that?"

"Yes, she liked that about him. She said his being married took the pressure off and she could just have fun. See, she wasn't looking to divorce John. Like I said earlier, my friend just needed—"

"Does the man have a name?" asked Peter, interrupting.

"I don't know. In fact, I insisted she not tell me. I felt guilty enough knowing what I did."

"So the only reason she stopped seeing him was the drinking. Is that right?" asked Lew.

"She also said she found out he was seeing someone else, too. Someone besides his wife. Margo has always been a health nut, so when she learned that she didn't like the possibility of being exposed to stuff. She called him 'a petri dish.'"

"So we've got a guy women find attractive who is a heavy drinker and plays around. Golly, Peter, Doc—how many guys do we know like that?" asked Lew, sounding grim. "A couple more questions, Robin, and I do appreciate you taking this time with us. This could be important. Do you know what kind of car he drove?"

"No, sorry. I only ever saw him that one day he rescued Margo and he was with his friend on the pontoon. The next time I saw him was in the bar that afternoon. I didn't pay much attention, I'm sorry."

"Did she indicate if he seemed angry at her cutting off their affair?"

"No. We didn't talk about it much. I was relieved but more worried about the new guy."

"And that person lives in Chicago?"

"Yes. But there is something you should know," said Robin, her voice dropping to a whisper. "John did find out about Margo and the fishing guy. I don't know how. Maybe he overheard a phone call, saw a text message, I'm not sure. But he knew and he was going to ask Margo for a divorce."

"And how do you know this?" asked Osborne.

"He told my husband. Jerry and I are the only people who

know this. Now, whether or not he was going to actually divorce her, who knows? Some couples are able to work stuff like that out though"—her voice dropped as she finished her sentence—"not many."

"And Margo?" asked Osborne. "Did she know her husband was aware of her involvement with another man?"

"He probably told her the night he got there."

"The night before he was killed."

"And she was killed," added Peter.

"Robin," said Lew, "an early theory of what happened that night at the Powers home has been murder-suicide. That was before the house and property were searched and no gun was found. Plus the angle of the gunshot wounds rules out any being self-inflicted. That's why we're looking for the person or persons who executed John and his wife.

"Thank you so much for your time," said Lew. "This has been very, very helpful."

"I don't know how," said Robin, her voice sad. "I wish *I* knew what happened that night. . . ."

"Thank you, Robin," added Osborne, "you've given us a better picture of your friend Margo, one that may lead us somewhere."

———

"Peter, what do you think?" asked Lew when Robin was off the phone.

"I think we search in two directions," said Peter. "Could still be a business deal gone bad, could be a love affair turned dangerous. I'm hesitant to put money on either right now."

# CHAPTER EIGHTEEN

Osborne was just off the phone when he heard a knock at the back door. In walked Mallory with Josh right behind her.

"Hey, Dad, how's it going?"

Osborne gave her a quick hug and pulled out the kitchen chairs. "Have a seat, you two. Been a busy morning out here on the lake. Just got off a conference call with Chief Ferris and one of the lawyers who works for John Powers's company. He thought we should talk to some of the people who knew the victims, the wife in particular, so we did and learned a few things."

"Anything you feel free to talk about?" asked Josh. "And sorry if I'm out of line asking you that. Being an investigative reporter, I'm afraid I ask w-a-a-a-y too many questions, especially about matters that are none of my business." He laughed.

Osborne chuckled, too. He was beginning to like the guy, even if he did look like he was twelve years old.

"I don't think what we learned has any real bearing on the murder case itself, unfortunately. The big news is the wife was having an affair. How often have you heard that story?"

"Umm," said Mallory, "some guy in Chicago? Hopefully

not her husband's best friend. That is one story I hear way too often. . . ."

"No, someone up here. Two guys out fishing rescued her when she fell out of her kayak and . . . well, apparently one guy never went home. The husband, John Powers, had just found out about it."

"Adds color to the story," said Mallory in a dry tone.

"I know," said Josh, "the cuckolded spouse hired a hit man to kill the lover but the lover paid off the hit man and—"

"It isn't funny, Josh," said Mallory, repressing a smile. She threw a look at Osborne, hoping he wasn't offended. "You watch too much TV."

"No. I cover too many divorces gone bad. Not really, sorry, Dr. Osborne, my sense of humor can be lacking sometimes."

"Not as bad as Ray's," said Mallory, widening her eyes. "You want inappropriate humor—"

"Hey! Who's using my name in vain?" said a familiar voice from the front porch where he had let himself in. "Oh, hi there, Josh. Speaking of humor—did you hear the one about the dyslexic man who walked into a bra?"

"Told you," said Mallory, shaking her head. "Disgusting. Really, Ray, would you tell your mother a joke like that?" She raised a hand as Ray opened his mouth. "No, don't answer, I know you would."

Pulling out the last empty chair, Ray folded his legs under the table and said, "Sorry I didn't knock, but you folks were arguing and I didn't want to ruin a close family moment."

"What? We aren't arguing. Dad was just telling us about the Powers murder—"

"Murder. I'll tell you who *I* want to murder," said Ray,

looking around him, as if to be sure the subject of his ire wasn't lurking nearby, "that woman."

"What woman are you talking about?" asked Mallory as she stood up and walked across the room to rummage in Osborne's refrigerator for a bag of raw carrots.

"Who do you think? Judith Kerr—the one, the only, the awful. Would you believe she has dropped by my place twice now: out of the blue, no warning, no phone call checking to see if I'm free. She must think I'm her default buddy system."

"C'mon, Ray, she's like all the girls—she thinks you're cute," said Mallory.

"Cute? Not me. No sirree, I am not her object of desire. Judy baby's got her hands all over Bill 'faithful husband' Kimble." Ray shivered as he stuck a hand into the bag of carrots that Mallory was holding out. "Man, that was one long afternoon guiding those two. She's rattling on about what a superhero she is—"

"She? Isn't Bill the superhero?" asked Mallory.

"Not this woman. She's been in the military, in the NSA, whatever the hell that is, the Special Forces, climbed Mount Everest. She might as well be saying 'anything you can do, I can do better.' You can't shut her up for all the bragging she does. Plus she's got sneaky hands and she's always watching. Like a goddamn turkey buzzard."

"The NSA?" asked Osborne. "That's the National Security Agency, one step beyond the CIA for national security and high-tech spying." As he spoke, he tried to remember where it was he had just heard someone else talk about the NSA. Was it Judith? He gave up. Maybe Lew would remember.

"Oh, come on, Ray, you're exaggerating," said Osborne. "Judith Kerr was not in the marines."

"No, and she didn't climb Mount Everest, either," said Ray, "but she did mention the NSA at least three times."

"Certainly makes her sound more interesting than placid little Evie," said Mallory through her carrot munching.

"Who's Evie?" asked Josh.

"Bill Kimble's perfectly pretty, perfectly nice, and serially betrayed wife who was his high school sweetheart," said Mallory. "They were the perfect couple: he was captain of the football team while she was prom queen, homecoming queen, and—"

"And boring as hell?" asked Josh. Osborne was definitely starting to like this guy.

"Kimble's no star conversationalist himself," said Mallory.

"How would *you* know?" asked Ray.

The three men stared at her.

"I took my turn getting hit on years ago," said Mallory, "and I knew right away that was not the direction I wanted to go. So there."

"At least you're honest, more than I can say for Judith. Geez."

"What does that mean?"

"Not much. She faked knowing how to cast so one of us, and I made sure it was Bill, would have to wrap his arms around the little lady and show her how. A little later I could see she knew exactly what she was doing. She can handle a boat and a spinning rod as well as anyone I know."

"Speaking of Bill Kimble," said Osborne, "seems Margo Powers had something going on the side with some fellow up here. Same kind of razzbonya as Bill: married and fooling around."

Pouring himself a fresh cup of coffee, Osborne said, "I knew the elder Kimbles. His father's office was next to mine and his mother was the receptionist. They were good people and doted on that boy. I just don't understand his behavior. I guarantee he did not learn it from his father."

After everyone nodded, humoring Osborne, Mallory spoke up. "C'mon, Dad, it's everywhere. Just go online, for heaven's sake, and see how many men—married men whom you may know—are on the dating sites, trolling for women. Sure, Bill Kimble plays around but he's one of dozens."

"It's that bad? Really?"

"Dad, you have never been in the game so how would you know? If you sat down with friends of mine, women who are looking to meet someone online *legitimately*, they will tell you they learn right away how to spot the bad actors. Bill Kimble is so obvious he's harmless."

"Okay, okay, I'm convinced," said Osborne, looking at his unexpected visitors. "On another subject, have I missed something? Why are you guys here?"

"Oh, right, sorry, Dad. Ray's taking Josh and I out to the sandbar again."

"I've got a spinning rod all set for you, Josh," said Ray. "Ready to go find fish? Mallory, ready?"

And with that the three walked through Osborne's living room to the porch and disappeared out the door. He could still hear their chatter when his phone rang. Lew was on the line.

"Slight change of plans, Doc. I had planned to take Bruce

fishing on Wednesday, thinking we might have gotten through critical stages of the Powers investigation, but his lab called to say they won't have results for another day or so. Plus we have the Kudelik case, and those results are pending, too. He and I talked and decided to sneak out late morning tomorrow for a few hours. Head for the Prairie River. Are you in?"

"Try leaving without me."

"Good. I'll get in touch with that Diane Armeo who's got the team working on the cybersecurity project next door to my place. See if she wants to join us."

# CHAPTER NINETEEN

How did I get so lucky? thought Osborne from his sliver of the front seat where he was wedged between the passenger-side door of Lew's fishing truck and Diane Armeo.

As they bounced over the rutted lane leading to the clearing where they could park, Lew said, "Doc, I'm turning you loose to work on that double-haul while I get Diane started. Keep an eye out for Bruce, will you, please? He was to meet us out here as soon as he wrapped up a meeting with two FBI agents working on the Powers case."

"Got it," said Osborne as he climbed out of the old pickup that Lew had inherited from her grandfather years ago. How she kept it running was a testament to the elderly mechanic who lived over in Tomahawk and had worked on the truck back when her grandfather was still alive.

Osborne liked to kid her that when "old Harry dies, you won't be able to find a mechanic with the tools needed to work on a truck this ancient." Every time he said it, he got the dim eye. He loved it when she did that.

His fly rod resting on his shoulder, he followed the two women down to the bank of the Prairie. "This is a *river?*" asked Diane, sounding skeptical.

"That's the official name," said Lew. "Were you expecting the Mississippi?"

Diane smiled sheepishly and shrugged.

"The Prairie is one of Wisconsin's finest trout streams," said Lew, "known for its native brook trout. A hundred years ago, the brookies in here were much larger than the eight- to ten-inchers we'll see today. If it weren't for 'catch-and-release,' which means fishermen don't keep and eat these trout, they might be gone. Small though they are, brook trout are fun to fish—and they are gorgeous to look at. You'll see what I mean."

As Lew studied the water they were about to enter, a wide smile broke across her face. "Doc, do you see what I'm seeing? A terrific blue-wing olive hatch." She turned toward Osborne and Diane, who were watching her, and said, "We couldn't have a better day. Just look at the spinners."

A puzzled look on her face, Diane asked, "Wait—olives? What do olives have to do with fly-fishing?" She had a clipped no-nonsense way of speaking.

"Blue-wing olive is the name we give to a mayfly—the insect you see spinning over the water," said Lew. "Brook trout love 'em."

———

Osborne had noted that with her short dark brown hair, plain features with no makeup in sight, and a sturdy figure clad in jeans and a worn gray T-shirt that had WASHINGTON NATIONALS emblazoned on the front, Diane reminded him of Lew. Though it was clear that the two women were just getting to know each other, their conversation struck him as comfortable, straightforward.

Of course, as their instructor Lew was the voice of authority this morning, but Diane, in from the East Coast and with an impressive government résumé, might have been intimidating. Then again, Osborne had never seen Lew intimidated by anyone. Certainly not by him. Or Bruce. Or by any of the people she interacted with who had academic credentials far exceeding her own.

---

Leaving Lew to introduce Diane to the challenges of casting a fly rod, Osborne stepped off the bank to wade upstream. "Today's the day," he muttered to himself. He was determined to master the goddamn double-haul if it killed him. It wasn't the double-haul that threatened his life; it was the Prairie that might get him when he was concentrating so hard on arm movements that he forgot to watch his feet.

The river bottom wasn't smooth and easy to wade like rivers in the photos he had seen of trout water in magazines. The Prairie was hollowed out in places hard to see with deep holes carved by the currents, the holes always changing, never in the same place. He had learned the hard way to take each step with caution, checking the rocky bottom beneath his waders, anxious to avoid a surprise drop-off.

Tearing his eyes away from the hazards below, he looked up. The azure sky was studded with alabaster swaths of cotton candy. Now that made the risk of falling worth it. Inhaling happily, Osborne waded on, frustration fading for the moment, his heart as light as the early summer breeze.

After wading up and around a bend, he paused, pleased with the vista before him: room to cast, not too many branches reaching to capture his fly line. Yes, the perfect spot. Bracing himself against the current, he tied on his favorite dry fly, the #16 Adams. He checked his tippet, his leader, his fly line. All was ready.

*He* was ready. Today he would do it, today he would master what Lew called "the dance": that smooth shift of weight forward and back, of line hand and rod hand moving in opposition, and shooting his line in two casts. Just two. Today he would do it. He would, he would, he would. He cast, he double-hauled . . . kind of.

"D-o-o-c, remember what I told you," said a familiar voice. He hadn't heard Lew coming. "You're doing better, but keep working. Remember, your goal is to shoot all your line in just two casts. And use a weight shift on each cast."

I *know* that, thought Osborne, what the hell do you think I'm trying to do? Setting his jaw, he kept his frustration to himself.

After delivering more instructions, ones that he had heard many times before, Lew and Diane moved past him a few yards. "Bruce should be here any minute," said Lew, climbing out of the water and onto the bank, where she sat down on a hillock of grass. "Diane, you go up ahead and practice that roll cast. Remember to lift from the shoulder—don't swing outward."

Five minutes hadn't passed when Osborne heard waders pushing through the current. Nothing about Bruce was ever quiet. Certainly not this morning.

"Chief," he called the second he caught sight of Lew. "Check this out. You gotta see my new Winston Boron IIIX three-weight. Just got it last week, and man, it should be perfect for the Prairie right here. It's designed for small creeks and streams, right?" He cast and caught his fly in a low-hanging branch.

As he waded over to untangle it, Lew said, "I wish we had talked before you spent all that money. Short rods sound like a good idea but they demand more of the caster. Bruce, you'll need longer strokes and more speed—not to mention precise timing. But maybe you just learned that." Osborne repressed a grin; Lew could be blunt.

"I know, I know, but that's why I fish with you," said Bruce, giving her a big grin, his bushy eyebrows hiked high in good humor. He waded off a short distance and cast again. This time he did not snag his fly but it landed with quite a disturbing *plop*. Bruce looked worried.

"Hey, you'll get better," said Lew, encouraging him. "This is your first day out with this rod, so take it easy."

"But what should I do?" asked Bruce, sounding more like a frustrated fourth-grader than a talented forensic scientist.

"First things first," said Lew, getting to her feet to demonstrate. "Do this: forget the rod size and do what I've taught you when we're fishing the Prairie, which is to shorten your cast and work your way up the run. You want that deep, sheltered pool"—she pointed as she was talking—"right there where you know that clever son of a bitch is hiding. So keep your casts under twenty feet and see if you can sneak it past those branches, treacherous devils."

She and Osborne watched in silence as Bruce tried one, then another cast. "Getting better," said Lew, though Osborne didn't see any improvement.

Bruce turned around to look at them. "I'm hungry."

"You just got here." Lew laughed. She could see Diane farther up the stream and waved to her. "Lunchtime," she called.

Wading toward them and holding her borrowed fly rod high, Diane said, "I love this. I love fly-fishing. I can't believe I haven't done this before."

———————

Over the bologna sandwiches, baby carrots, and potato chips that Lew had packed along for everyone, the four of them chatted. Just off the bank, the mayflies spun, the fish slurped, and Lew urged everyone to eat fast. "This hatch could disappear any moment," she said.

"So, Diane," said Bruce, talking with his mouth full after Lew had introduced them, "I hear you're with the NSA and you're after those hackers from Russia?"

Diane's face changed. The relaxed smiles that had crossed her face as she chatted and gulped down a sandwich disappeared. Her shoulders stiffened and, turning away, she got to her feet and walked her used napkin and plastic wrap over to the trash bag by Lew.

With an audible sigh, she turned to Bruce. "Mr. Peters," she said, using his last name to make a point, "because you are in law enforcement, I will answer your questions—briefly. And no more after this, agreed?"

Looking mollified, Bruce nodded his agreement.

"I am a private contractor and colleagues of mine are monitoring the hackers who took over the computer belonging to Chief Ferris's neighbors. That is all I wish to say on that matter," said Diane.

"Question two—you are wrong on the NSA. I left government service last year to cofound a cybersecurity firm. So I'm a civilian, Bruce, and please honor the fact I would like to keep our work here as confidential as possible. If anyone asks, I recommend you say we're exploring fiber-optic opportunities and leave it at that."

"Will do," said Bruce. "Not a problem, and sorry if I offended you. Funny thing, though," said Bruce, "something you might like to know. Doc's neighbor Ray Pradt was just telling me about this woman who's new in town and keeps bugging him to take her fishing. She was with the NSA, too.

"Again, not to offend you"—Bruce raised his eyebrows in apology this time—"but how the hell often does that happen? Two spies in little Loon Lake at the same time."

"*I am not a spy.*" Diane's face froze, her eyes turned steely, and she gave Bruce a deadening look, a look that reminded Osborne of the wolf that had confronted him on a deer trail two years ago. He might have been a six-foot-two-inch man with a gun that day, but he had known in his gut that a move other than backing up and climbing safely into his car would be a mistake.

Bruce shuddered. He got the message. He made a pretense of looking for his fly rod and fussing with the reel. Diane watched him for a moment before asking, "And who is this person you're referring to?"

"I think he's talking about Judith Kerr," said Osborne, hoping to save Bruce some embarrassment. "Originally a local person, she grew up in Loon Lake but has been gone for years. Apparently she just moved back. My neighbor whom he mentioned is a muskie guide who attracts women whether he wants to or not."

"He's certainly not fond of that one," said Bruce with a roll of his eyes and happy to say something more acceptable. "Not to hear him tell."

"Judith can be a bit much," said Osborne, gathering up his own napkin and empty water bottle. "She grew up next door to our family when we lived in town, and she didn't have the easiest childhood, so I'd cut her some slack." He threw a look at Bruce, encouraging him to drop the subject. The day was too nice to go on about Judith Kerr.

"Thank you, Dr. Osborne," said Diane, sounding grateful that he could see she wanted to end that conversation.

"So, Chief," said Diane, "what do you recommend I do if I want to learn more about fly-fishing when I go back east? Any books you recommend? Videos?"

"I'm glad you asked," said Lew, holding out a paper sack for everyone to put their garbage in. "For one thing, you will have to make a choice, and it's one that's personality-driven. Do you want to go technical, like our friend Bruce here? Or be more of a generalist, like me. And Doc."

"Do you mean I'm doing things all wrong?" asked Bruce, sounding wounded.

"Not at all," said Lew. "When it comes to fly-fishing, some people love the detail you can get into: study all the insect patterns, learn to tie trout flies, immerse yourself in all the science and preparation that goes with fly-fishing. Then there is learning casting technique and fly-fishing gear and . . ."

"Are you trying to tell me a person can obsess over this sport?" Diane gave a happy snort.

"Yes. I'll show you what I mean," said Lew. "Bruce, show her the trout flies you have on you right now. All of them."

With a sheepish grin, Bruce reached into one pocket after another on his fishing vest until he had pulled out six plastic containers, each holding numerous trout flies.

"And how many do I have?" Lew asked with a smile as she reached into her vest pocket for one small clear plastic box. "I have exactly eight flies: I have four Adamses in sizes twelve, fourteen, sixteen, and eighteen. But all I have besides my Adams flies are one Royal Wulff, one Pale Morning Dun, and one very colorful Salmon Stone Fly. That's all. Usually I only have one Adams, but I had a hunch we might have this blue-wing olive hatch today and I wanted to be covered."

"Whew. Going back to my first question," said Diane, "where do I start?"

"When you return to the East Coast, I suggest you do what I did five years ago, even though I had been fly-fishing by the seat of my pants for years: go to the Wulff School of Fly Fishing in the Catskills. There is no better place in the country to learn.

"They will teach you everything from insects and water to trout flies to equipment. Most important, they will teach you how to cast and help you find the fly rod just right for you. I went for a long weekend and I don't know of a better way to treat yourself. One of these days I hope to go back."

"Damn," said Bruce, "I should go."

"Right now, you're going back in the water, everyone," said Lew, shooing them off the grass. "I see brookies slurping. . . ."

She was right. The water was active with happy fish. Osborne scrambled his way into the stream and waded a short distance before he was ready to cast. As he moved with the double-haul, he mulled over the idea of the Wulff School of

Fly Fishing. Hmm, maybe he should go, maybe he could talk Lew into going with him . . . humm.

"Oh, my gosh, Doc! You did it. That was a perfect double-haul." Lew was shouting from thirty yards downstream.

Osborne straightened up and cast again. Damn, this felt good.

"You took your mind off the mechanics, I'll bet," said Lew, who had waded closer.

"I did," said Osborne, too thrilled to say more.

Lew's personal cell phone buzzed. She looked down. "It's Ray," she said as she answered and listened. "I'm sorry to hear this. Are you okay?"

Osborne stood still, listening.

"I'll be right there. Got Bruce and Doc with me. Don't let anyone near the body or the area until we get there. No, Ray, don't worry about photos. Wait right there."

Off her phone, Lew closed her eyes and pressed the fingers of her right hand against her eyelids for a long moment before she said, her voice cracking, "Sorry, Doc, no more fishing today. They found Lillian Curran's body."

# CHAPTER TWENTY

Osborne pulled in behind Lew's truck and hurried behind her down the town road that led past two large homes set back from the road to a third driveway, which led to a similar large home. On the way into town from the Prairie River she had let him off at the police station to get his car before driving straight to the location Ray had given them.

Just before the third driveway was a low barbed wire fence that appeared to have been put up in haste or by someone who didn't know what they were doing. The top section had been rolled or pushed down. Ray's truck was parked across the road from the fence and behind a small sedan that Osborne recognized as belonging to Lillian Curran. On the side of the road by the fence was a Loon Lake Police squad car.

About fifty yards in from the road and along a path marked by the barbed wire, Osborne could see Ray standing with Officer Donovan and a man with a dog. "I'll follow you," he said to Lew, and fell in behind her.

"What's the story?" Lew asked the group as they neared. Ray stepped forward. "Art Mason here"—he pointed to a man whom Osborne didn't know—"was walking his dog and trying to keep him from getting tangled up in all this barbed wire some idiot strung along here—"

"A property dispute between the Kimbles, who live over there," said Officer Donovan, interrupting, "and the people on this side."

"Right," said Ray, "so Art's dog started going crazy out on the road and he decided to walk him back this way—"

"When we found the body," said Art. "She's been here a while, I think. By the way, I live about five houses down the road," he said, stepping forward to introduce himself to Lew and Osborne. "I walk Chipper here every day and for the last four or five days, he's been skittish right along the road here. I hesitated to walk in 'cause I might be trespassing, but I was curious. Figured it was probably a dead bear or something."

"I should have known," said Ray, his hands thrust deep into the pockets of his fishing shorts. "I should have driven around and looked for Lillian's car. Dammit." He raised his right forearm to cover his eyes as his shoulders shook. Osborne walked closer to him and rubbed his shoulders.

"Ray," he said in a low voice, "how would you have known? This is a couple miles from her place. No one would know to look for her over here."

"What on earth?" Lew was shaking her head, puzzled. "Why would Lillian be back in here? What the hell—" Lew looked hard around the area where they were standing. She took a step forward.

"Careful, Chief," said Officer Donovan, who had been standing back, listening, "the body is just over there."

"Todd," said Lew, in a harsh tone, "I can tell, thank you."

"Yeah, that's the smell of something dead," said Art. "I heard the Kimble dogs got away from Evie this morning, but the fence was still up and they got pretty badly cut. When I heard that, I came down here with my wire cutters and pulled it back. Didn't need that happening to Chipper."

"How long has this fence been up?" asked Lew. "Is it permanent?"

"Oh, no. The people who just moved in here, the Tolberts, think Bill Kimble put his driveway on their property. They put the fence up two days ago until the county takes a look to see who's right."

"That may help us determine how long Lillian's been lying here," said Lew.

Just then Bruce drove up in his SUV. He came bustling over and stopped short of the group. "Oh, oh, what's happened here?"

"We're not sure exactly," said Lew, "so far all we know is we've found the remains of a missing person. An elderly lawyer named Lillian Curran."

Bruce looked uncomfortable for a minute, then brightened as he said, "Dr. Osborne, you're the acting coroner if I'm not mistaken. Looks to me like the next job is yours."

Everyone except Ray gave Osborne a look of sympathy for the job he had ahead of him.

"I don't mind," said Osborne, rebuffing their hints. "I've been hunting long enough there's no surprises. Plus she was a patient of mine, someone I've always been very fond of."

"And mine, a special friend of mine," said Ray, wiping at his face. "Let's do it, Doc."

The two men walked toward a birch tree with branches hanging over a faint path. On the path lay a small figure lying facedown. The body was wrapped in a maroon jacket. "Wait here, Ray," said Osborne, "I need to get my medical bag from the car."

---

Minutes later, kneeling over what remained of Lillian, Osborne paused. He was no pathologist, so nothing was needed from him except to determine that the victim was deceased and a likely cause of death. He had approached the corpse assuming Lillian had died of a heart attack or a stroke. After all, the woman was ninety, but what he saw was disturbing.

"Bruce," he said, looking down, "you're wrong. This is your job, my good man."

"What?" Bruce hurried over.

With one of his instruments, Osborne pointed in the direction of Lillian's head. "The jaw is shattered," he said, indicating shards of bone and tooth. "This is not caused by a scavenging animal—this is caused by a bullet . . . or two."

"Are you sure?" asked Bruce.

"I am, but your pathologist can confirm it." He glanced up at Bruce and Ray. "I guarantee Lillian Curran did not die a natural death."

"But who would shoot an old woman?" asked Art Mason, who had tied his dog to a tree before walking over.

"She was a retired trial lawyer," said Lew. "Could be someone who lost a case to her?"

"She was hated by birders," said Ray in a quiet voice. "She was proud of that."

"Are you serious?" asked Lew. "I've never heard of angry birders and I've heard of, about, and from plenty of angry people."

"She was telling me last week that she has been watching this great horned owl until two or three in the morning. She didn't say where but she found his perch, she said, and loved to watch and listen to him.

"But birders are very interested in owls, so after she posted on a birding site that she had observed this one particular owl shrieking to protect its nest, she had legions of people bugging her to tell them where she saw it, and she refused to tell them. Two people even drove up from Chicago and knocked on her door, demanding she show them where the owl had its nest. She refused.

"And if you knew my friend Lillian, she could refuse in a pretty unpleasant way."

"Still, no reason to shoot her," said Lew.

"No, I agree," said Ray. Osborne, Bruce, Officer Donovan, and Art Mason also agreed, though they seemed a little uncertain.

"Ray," said Lew, putting an arm around him, "are you in any condition to take part in searching the property here for any trace of who might have killed Lillian? I know it's a lot to ask right now. . . ."

"On one condition," said Ray, straightening up and with eyes so sad and determined that Osborne wondered if he had ever seen such an expression on his friend's face. Maybe once, the time he hitched a plow onto the front of his pickup and drove in the middle of the night through a blizzard to get Osborne's late wife to the hospital when her bronchitis had turned deadly.

"Is it legal for me to conduct the search for no payment?" asked Ray. "I want to do this for Lillian. Not for the town, the county, not for anyone except my dear friend." And he walked away before anyone could see him cry.

"Not a problem," said Lew, calling after him. "Officer Donovan knows the protocol for establishing the crime scene. He'll take care of that."

"My people will handle the body when it's time," said Bruce quietly. He had been standing a distance away, his back turned, and murmuring in low tones on his cell phone.

———————

An hour later Lew walked into the police station still wearing her fishing shorts and khaki shirt. Marlaine, who was on Dispatch, stood up and made Lew come around the desk for a sympathetic hug. "Everyone knew that crabby old lady," said Marlaine, half joking and half crying herself. "I called her 'old Loon Lake.' "

"She was that, all right," said Lew, picking up a few messages that Marlaine had set aside for her. She looked down at the slips of paper. "Kara Kudelik's dad?"

"He's called three, four times. I had to discourage him from coming over and waiting for you. Put him at the top of your list."

———————

"Chief Ferris?" asked the gruff voice on the phone. "You won't believe what I came across. I think I have a good idea who killed my daughter."

"I see. Is this something you and I could go over first thing tomorrow morning?"

"No. I'm parked out in front of your police station. I'll be right there."

With a sigh of fatigue, Lew told Marlaine to go ahead and send him back, then she put down her phone and waited.

"Here, I've got the letter with me," said Bernie Kudelik as he charged into her office. He threw a piece of notebook paper on which a parent of one of Kara's students had written:

> *I know you hate my son. I know you have no qualifications to be teaching ninth grade. You of all teachers should recognize a student who is too smart for your backward curriculum. My Steven is smarter than any stupid kid in your class and you know it. Just you wait—you flunk him once more and I'LL TAKE CARE OF YOU.*

"This is dated two days before Kara was murdered," said her angry father. "Two days. Just two days. I think we know who—"

"Is there a name on this, Bernie?" Lew studied the sheet of paper.

"No, but I found out who the 'Steven' is in her class. I looked up the parents' address. I have it right here. I drove by their house, too. Their cars are in the driveway. You can arrest them right now."

"Oh, it's not that easy, Bernie. I'll need to look into this further, talk with the district attorney. I don't blame you for thinking these people may be involved, but frankly, teachers get notes like this from angry parents often. This doesn't mean they killed your daughter."

"I think you're wrong."

"Bernie," said Lew, standing up and walking over to him, "you have the Wausau Crime Lab experts poring over the evidence we've found at Kara's house. They have a lead and we need to give them time to work it. Just stay calm and trust us, please?"

"What's the lead?"

"Still confidential but I will tell you as soon as it's confirmed. So please go home and know we're following up on that and I will share this letter with the forensic techs, too."

"Good. They can match the DNA," said Bernie.

When Lew was able to shuffle him out the door, assured he wouldn't knock on the door of the parents of the bad-behaving ninth-grader, she muttered to herself, "Too much TV. People like Bernie watch too much TV. They think DNA is everywhere, for God's sake."

# CHAPTER TWENTY-ONE

Examining the ground cover and nearby shrubs surrounding Lillian's still form with the same instinct he used to track a twelve-point buck, Ray kept in mind the appearance of the shattered jaw. He made a number of guesses at possible trajectories of the bullets that did the damage.

While debating what would have caused the bone to shatter in the direction it did, he reminded himself this was the body of an elderly woman whose bones were likely to be exceptionally brittle.

Next, he studied the periphery of the site where Lillian's body had dropped when she died. Several times he paused to check overhead, as he imagined she must have done while searching for a glimpse of the great horned owl.

Before he stepped back to allow two of Bruce's forensic investigators to remove the body, he took photos of her shoes and the ground near her feet.

While he was doing so, one of the investigators said, "Be careful what you assume based on what you see around the body today. All these leaves and the ground cover may have been disturbed by the body as rigor mortis took hold and released."

"Good point," said Ray, "not to mention curious raccoons and all their cousins."

Even as Ray knew that the human remains being removed by the investigators no longer belonged to his dear friend, he had the sense that she was near, she was watching. Of that he was sure. He smiled at the odor of the decomposing flesh, knowing what he would say to Osborne later: "Lillian could be difficult in life and just as difficult in death. It was not easy to get close to her living or dead."

Once the parameters of the crime scene had been set, he walked the wider area, searching the ground beneath his feet, the brush, nearby tree trunks and overhanging branches. He had spotted the nest belonging to the great horned owl, so he had a good idea of where Lillian would have positioned herself to watch.

The evidence confirmed his theory: broken branches, crushed acorns, and torn leaves. But something else became obvious as he studied the patterns left by human presence: Lillian was not alone. Someone else had moved through there, too. Someone heavier, taller, and wearing a shoe that left an impression in the moist soil under a clump of ferns—a footprint he was able to document with his camera and with the eyes he had trained since childhood.

---

Ray was eight years old when he met the old trapper who lived in a shack down a fire lane that his grandfather had shown him. The old man sold raspberries he harvested from an ancient patch on his land, berries only a few people knew about.

Ray's grandfather, a retired doctor, knew about them because he had traded the old man "berries for bee stings" after the old man had stumbled onto a wasp nest and nearly died from anaphylactic shock.

That summer Ray loved to ride his bike out to the old man's place. There he would follow him around, listening to his stories as he learned to track beaver and deer, even bear and other creatures that lived hidden in the forests.

Eventually, trusting the boy was genuinely interested, the elderly trapper introduced him to his friends, other old men who, like him, had once made a living trapping beaver and squirrel, rabbit and mink. Some were Native American, others from Russia, Croatia, and Norway. Given their eager audience, they settled in to tell stories and share what they had learned from the generations of trappers and hunters who preceded them.

Ray never forgot what they had taught him. In his late teens, as he hunted alongside his father and his father's deer camp buddies, he became known as one of the finest trackers in the northwoods.

Today his dad's hunting buddies who were still alive but now retired and meeting mornings at McDonald's for coffee, would commiserate about Ray, saying, "That razzbonya's got the eyes of an eagle. Too bad he can't package and sell it."

They were wrong. Ray's talent might not be one he could make money on like that of a doctor, a lawyer, or an entrepreneur. But it was a talent that had made for him a rich life, a life he loved, a life that made him happy.

---

The great horned owl's nest was set high in a red pine surrounded by a mix of birch and oak. The afternoon sunlight made it easy for Ray to scan nearby tree trunks, hoping that whoever shot Lillian had fired more than once. Stepping closer to a birch tree, which would have been to Lillian's left as she stood gazing up at the red pine, he found what he was looking for: two bullet holes. He marked the holes so one of the Wausau boys could find the depressions left by the bullets. Reaching for his cell phone, he called Bruce to put bullet recovery on his list.

As he resumed his search, he was aware that he was walking over properties belonging to different owners. Lillian had been found on the land belonging to Bill Kimble and his wife; the property to the south belonged to their new neighbors, the ones who had rigged up the barbed wire while disputing the property line. As of the discovery of Lillian Curran's body and under Lew's direction, the barbed wire had been rolled up and returned to its owner.

Walking along a deer path running between the two properties, Ray noticed again that someone other than Lillian had walked through there recently. Stepping farther onto the Kimble land, he found himself in a small clearing. At first, he thought deer had been bedding down there, but a close examination showed a human being had visited the location a number of times.

A birder, of course, he thought, once he realized that the spot had been visited numerous times by the same individual. He was about to return to the site where Lillian's body had been found when he spotted something white under a young balsam: a used Kleenex.

He didn't touch it. Instead he called Bruce once more.

"Hey, can you get someone out here right away? I found a used Kleenex left by someone other than the old lady. It's a good fifty feet from where we found Lillian, but I can tell someone has been hanging around here. Another birder, maybe, but it could also be someone who saw something the night Lillian was killed.

"I don't want to touch it," said Ray. "Your people know how to handle evidence like this better than me."

"Good find," said Bruce. "If you'll wait for me, I'll be there in few minutes. I was on my way out to the Kudelik crime scene but that can wait."

———

It was dusk before two of Bruce's investigators had finished removing the spent bullets from the tree and pored over every inch of the clearing where Ray had found the used Kleenex. That item had been slipped into an evidence envelope and was on its way to the lab for DNA testing.

After putting his cameras back in the pickup, Ray walked back for one more look at the place where Lillian had died. He retraced his steps from earlier in the day as the sense of Lillian's presence still lingered. He sat down on a stump, took a deep breath, and closed his eyes.

As he sat there, night falling, he thought back over the days when he had been checking Lillian's house and hoping to see that she had returned. Thought back over the delightful conversations he'd had over the years with the eccentric old woman. Then he remembered all the bluegills he had brought her and smiled to himself as the thought reminded him he was hungry.

Opening his eyes, he got to his feet. A whisper of wings and the great horned owl whooshed at his face. He ducked. When he looked up, the bird was gone, only the moon hung in the sky where seconds before fierce eyes had startled him.

He was about to walk back to his truck when he saw a bright light shining through the trees. As he watched, standing near the spot where Lillian had died, he could see a figure, a woman, moving in front of the light. It took a moment for him to recognize the figure and the place: he was watching Evie Kimble in her kitchen. As he watched, he wondered: Could she be seen every night around this same time? From this same spot?

He thought of the clearing, of the tracks he had found of someone lingering there. He retraced his steps to the clearing. Yes. Standing here he had an even better view of the interior of the Kimble kitchen and the woman who lived there.

He looked down at the pattern of leaves and twigs around his feet. Pulling out his phone, he took half a dozen photos of the small clearing. In the fading light, the quality wasn't what Lew and the Wausau boys would need to make a court case but good enough that if he came back in the morning he would know if someone had been here.

As he turned in a circle, he wondered if he was making an absurd guess. But the longer he stood in the shadows, the more certain he was that he was onto something.

Ray knew a hiding place when he saw one, and this had the wrong sightlines for a birder stalking the great horned owl. This was for a watcher . . . watching.

But who? And why?

# CHAPTER TWENTY-TWO

Osborne took his usual seat at the oblong table in McDonald's. Four of his friends were already there sipping their morning coffees. Conversation stopped as he sat down and four pairs of eyes fixated on him, waiting.

"C'mon, Doc," said Herb Dickson, his oldest friend in the group, "what's the latest on our chances of being the next murder victims?" He gave a weak laugh, and Osborne smiled. He didn't blame his coffee buds for assuming he would have the most up-to-date news and not just because he was acting coroner. They knew with whom he shared a bed three times a week or more.

Osborne had to admit he enjoyed making them wait while he sipped from his cup of hot coffee once, twice. Then he gave in.

"Right now, I know what you know," he said, "but Chief Ferris has called a staff meeting for nine this morning, and I'm sure I'll hear something then. I hope."

"Heard on TV last night they found old Lillian," said Harry Madson in his low, grumpy voice. "Heart, you think?"

"Harry, we don't know yet," said Osborne. He had decided when Lew first asked him to help with investigations because of his forensic dentistry skills that any reports relative to crimes had to come first from her. Always.

While they were chatting, Gary Sandvik, a recently re-tired ophthalmologist, sat down. Gary was new to the group, having been a regular for only a year now. "Oh, hello guys," he said, pulling out a chair. "What have I missed?"

"Not a thing," said Herb, "talking to this guy's like pulling teeth—sorry, Doc."

"You don't sound sorry," said Osborne. "Look, fellas, all I can say is Lillian's body was found on the Kimble property, not far from their driveway and about a hundred feet in from the road. Know where I mean?"

"I know Kimble," said Gary. "Used to see that honking big black Range Rover of his parked at my neighbor's all the time—you know, the Powers place."

"You live next to the Powers mansion out there on Spider Lake?" asked Osborne. "When did you move out there? I thought you lived over in McNaughton."

"You're thinking of my brother-in-law," said Gary. "My wife and I built our home while I was still working, moved in last summer. Amazing, you know. Our place cost close to a million bucks, we live there year-round, while Powers spent at least ten mil on his and lives there only six weeks a summer. That's as much time he spends at the place. His wife is there more often . . . *was* there, I mean."

"How do you know that Range Rover belongs to Bill Kim-ble?" asked Osborne.

"Who else spends the money to have a license plate read 'PKRS'?" said Gary, hooting as he spoke.

"I didn't realize he was good friends with Bill Kimble," said Osborne. "That's an odd pair."

"Bill? Who said 'Bill'?" Gary hooted again.

Osborne took two more sips of his coffee, excused himself, walked out of McDonald's, and hurried down the street and across the wide green lawn to Lew's office with Gary's comment on rewind in his brain: "Bill? Who said 'Bill'?"

Lew was already seated in one of the chairs near the tall front windows that looked out across the courthouse lawn. The sunny June morning gave her office a warm glow. Bruce was there, too, sorting through a small stack of eight-by-ten photos.

Osborne was about to tell them both what he had just heard when Lew waved for him to sit. "Hold on for a few minutes, Doc," she said. "Bruce has an update for us that we should hear before anything else." She gave him a look that convinced him that even if he was trying to announce the end of the world, silence was a good option.

Osborne nodded, took the chair, and shut up.

"I am happy to say we have an excellent lead from the crime scene at the Powers home," said Bruce, laying out a color photo. "If you remember, a rainstorm had passed through the night before the bodies were found, leaving the lawn and landscaped areas around the house soaked, especially the dirt path leading from the kitchen's back door down to the dog kennel.

"That's where we found these prints of a woman's New Balance cross-trainer shoe." He handed the photo to Lew and Osborne. "That door, as it turns out, was rarely locked by the owners because they used it to let the dogs in and out. We think the shooter may have hid outside waiting for Margo and John Powers to return home that evening and then let herself in through the unlocked door."

"Wouldn't the dogs have alerted them to someone hiding out there?"

"You'd think so," said Bruce, "and we checked on that but turns out there is a bear that has been sighted in the yards of nearby homes. The dogs may have gone crazy and the Powerses just assumed it was the bear or a raccoon or some other critter. A heck of a lot of deer around there, too. But this isn't all. . . ."

He reached for another photo, again showing footprints. "We found these on the path leading down to Kara Kudelik's dock. Apparently she had watered grass she had been trying to grow in her backyard and that had left the path soaking wet."

He waited quietly while everyone studied the second photo.

"Similar footprint?" asked Lew.

"Yes, but this one is so clear that we could even get the size. Again, we've got a woman's New Balance cross-trainer shoe, size nine."

"Don't a lot of women wear those shoes?" asked Osborne, vaguely recalling seeing New Balance shoes on either Mallory or Erin. "One of my daughters does."

"Margo Powers did not own any. We checked. She wore K-Swiss. Kara Kudelik wore Nike," said Bruce. "But we've got evidence here that may allow us to confirm an identity of a suspect. The odd thing is that I don't see any connection between Kara Kudelik and John and Margo Powers. Not yet, anyway."

"Can I talk now?" asked Osborne with a slight smile and a questioning glance at Lew.

"Oh, wait," said Bruce, waving his hand, "I just want to add that we have nothing new from the authorities working in Evanston and Chicago regarding any strong leads on their end. They're still hoping to find someone or something connected to all the lawsuits John Powers was involved in."

"Except for one interesting development," said Osborne, "the fact his wife appears to have been having an affair with someone up here."

"Right," said Bruce. "I should have mentioned that, I guess."

"Well," said Osborne, "I have some very interesting information along that line. Gary Sandvik, who lives down the road from the Powers place, mentioned at coffee this morning that he was seeing a black Range Rover with a license plate reading 'PKRS' parked in the Powers driveway. . . ." Osborne, pleased with his little bombshell, sat back with a smug smile.

Lew and Bruce stared at him. Sounding confused, Bruce said, "So . . . some golf buddy of John's?"

"No," said Osborne. "Gary said he saw the Range Rover parked there when John Powers wasn't around, when Margo was staying there . . . alone."

"That's Bill Kimble's car," said Lew. "Are you implying?"

"How the hell would that guy you mentioned—Gary whoever—know if John Powers was in town or not?" asked Bruce. "Ever hear of people parking in their garage?"

Osborne gave him a long look. "Bruce, this is a small town.

I know Gary Sandvik and I know his wife and I know some other folks living down that road. Believe me, they all keep a close eye on one another. Since John Powers was known to spend only six weeks a summer in his multimillion-dollar residence, you can be sure his neighbors knew when he was coming and going.

"Add to that any suspicion among the neighbors as to what Margo might be up to and I'm sure she couldn't go to the grocery store without someone knowing," said Lew. "Gary's comment is worth looking into, but I can't see Bill Kimble as a person of interest in this. First of all, the guy may behave badly with women but he is hardly a homicidal maniac."

"No, of course not," said Osborne, "but it is worth knowing, don't you agree?"

"I still see no connection between the Powerses and Kara Kudelik," said Lew. "Nothing. Not only that, but I had to listen to a wacko theory from Kara's father that the parents of one of her students was so furious with how she treated their son that they killed her. He has an angry note he found in her desk"—Lew shook her head as she spoke—"so he jumped to a very emotional and angry conclusion.

"Right now, I'm hoping he doesn't do something unpleasant before we can clear this up. Bernie is a good man, but even good people can go a little nuts. . . ."

She looked so dejected, Osborne reached over to pat her hand.

A knock on the door and Lew turned, but before she could say a word, Ray burst into the room saying, "Whoever killed Lillian went back to a spot right near where we found her body sometime during the night last night. I checked this morning and I could see someone had been there after I left and I didn't leave until after ten last night. And I can see that this individual has been there before.

"Here's the thing. At first I thought it must be a birder looking for owls, but why are they standing in a clearing that gives you a sightline straight into the kitchen belonging to Bill and Evie Kimble? Could this be a stalker?"

"Ray, please sit down," said Lew, her eyes brightening. "We have two leads you should hear about and then we need a plan. Everyone, I feel like we're getting close to answers here, but that's all—just close. Bruce, you go first."

After the update on the footprints and news of Margo Powers's apparent affair with someone local, Ray said, "I am not sure if there is a connection between either of those cases and Lillian's death. Be helpful to know if the bullets dug from the tree near Lillian's body match the ones that killed John and Margo Powers, won't it."

"We'll know in a day or two," said Bruce. "I have a question for Ray. Going back to your comment that the person who returned to the area where Lillian was found and who could see into the Kimble family's kitchen, are they standing close enough that if they had a gun they might be within range of firing at someone in the house?"

"Possibly," said Ray. "That would depend on the type of rifle or handgun. A sniper would have an easy shot. That's what has me worried."

"It'll be interesting what we find on that used tissue you found yesterday afternoon," said Bruce. "If we get a DNA match on that, we'll have a person of interest in the death of Lillian Curran."

After Bruce and Ray left her office, Lew turned worried eyes to Osborne. "I wish we knew more about Kara Kudelik. Her father's theory that the parents of one of her students may have been furious enough to assault her does not make sense to me. But we don't know enough about the woman. Any suggestions?"

"Maybe," said Osborne. "Mallory was friends with Kara and they were in the same high school class. Why don't I see if Mallory knows if there's a close friend of Kara's to whom you could talk? If we could find out more about her personal life, we might make sense of some of this."

"Good idea, Doc. By the way, in our own homes tonight? I need to get my tomatoes planted and check on a few things."

"Oh, okay, if you insist," said Osborne, faking disappointment. "I'm kidding. You get those tomatoes planted and I'll check in with Mallory. Let you know what I find," said Osborne, giving her a peck on the cheek. "But I'll miss you."

She punched him in the arm and shoved him out her office door.

# CHAPTER TWENTY-THREE

Arriving home, Lew scrambled into her gardening clothes and rushed out to the raised beds in the pen at the back of her farmhouse. The twelve tomato plants that she had set out the previous Thursday before Suzanne and Becky arrived, before John and Margo Powers were murdered, before Lillian Curran disappeared, or, she was thinking, before all hell broke loose, were right where she had left them. Twelve innocent tomato plants waiting for a home.

Relieved that the plants appeared to be healthy, she started to dig, setting each plant four inches deep and sprinkling each hole with a dusting of fertilizer. In a few days, she would set wire cages around each one for support. She was so focused on her planting that she didn't hear the footsteps running toward her.

"Chief Ferris—" a voice shouted. Lew was so startled she flipped the trowel she was holding into the air. "Oh, I am so sorry," said Diane, peering through the deer fence.

"Golly, you startled me," said Lew, getting to her feet. "Hold on, Diane," she said with a welcoming smile, "I have some information on the Wulff School of Fly Fishing that I want to give you. It's sitting on my kitchen table. Have it for you in a sec."

"No, please, that's not why I came over," said Diane. "Can we walk down by the lake? I'd like to talk in private."

Lew glanced all around her. "There's no one here but me."

"Please," said Diane, looking at the woods surrounding Lew's farmhouse and her garden, "I'd like to keep this conversation between us, and if you're there and I'm here, I'll be shouting."

"I'm ready for a break, anyway," said Lew, pulling off her garden gloves and motioning for Diane to follow her down to the wrought iron bench on the shoreline next to her dock. "This is my favorite spot in the evening when the sun is going down behind those pines across the lake," she said as she made room for Diane to sit beside her.

"So what's up?" Lew studied the woman's face as she waited for her answer. She couldn't imagine anything wrong unless there was some issue with Diane's project next door. "Something I should know about your cyber pirates or my neighbors?" Lew was kidding, but she hoped she wouldn't be learning something awful about the people living next door.

"No, nothing like that. I ran a background check on the woman your friend mentioned. The one who has been telling people she's retired from the NSA."

"You must mean Judith Kerr. She's the one our friend Ray Pradt, the fishing guide, can't stand."

"That's the one. I was taken aback when it was mentioned that she had been with the NSA. It's unusual for people working within the agency or retired to talk about their work.

Not even our families know what we do. We say that we're with the Foreign Service or another agency, if only to protect colleagues who may still be active.

"Because our work often involves covert operations, it's crucial that we keep our connections quiet. The only reason you know that I was with the NSA is because our mutual colleague with the FBI cybersecurity team felt you needed to know. Frankly, I'm not sure he did the right thing, either. So you can see why I was curious as to when and where this Judith Kerr worked at the agency."

"And why she makes such a big deal about it?" asked Lew.

"Yes. Chief Ferris, that woman has had no connection to the NSA whatsoever, never has."

"Oh, so she's lying to impress people?" Lew snorted. "Funny how things change. Used to be women had cosmetic surgery to make themselves look better. Now they brag about their executive status in the business world. Instead of 'rock, paper, scissors' we've got 'brains beat beauty.'" Lew chuckled at her joke until she saw that Diane wasn't smiling.

"What I learned about the woman is enough to make you want to keep an eye on her. She's up to something."

"So you don't think she's simply moved back to where she grew up like many people do?"

"You tell me what you think after I tell you the rest of what I've learned," said Diane, gazing out across the calm water as she spoke. "First, she has a history of getting intimately involved with one or more of the men she reported to in two different corporations where she had been hired as a senior manager. Hired after faking her credentials."

"Meaning?"

"Meaning twice she was found to be having affairs with men she reported to and—"

"Diane," said Lew, "not to defend her, because I've only seen the woman once, but why would that be *her* fault?"

"That's not the end of the story," said Diane, "let me finish.

"In the first case, which was five years ago in Kansas City, when the man's wife learned what was going on and made a big stink, Judith was fired *and* her boss-lover told her to get out of his life. For two years following that episode, the married couple received threatening letters and obscene phone calls, which could never be traced to Judith, though they were sure it was her. They filed a police report, which is how I know this.

"In the second case, just a year ago in Minneapolis, she was again fired after an affair with a senior executive, who was also married. Shortly after she was fired and the boyfriend ended the relationship, a police report was filed alleging that both the man involved and his soon-to-be-estranged wife were being stalked. Again, no one was caught but the complaint named Judith Kerr as a suspect.

"And the last point I want to make is this: my background check showed an erratic career path where she would be hired as a senior manager but last only a year or two before moving on to a new job. I suspect she has always doctored her résumé, and recruiters are notorious for not running thorough background checks. Add to that the fact that people give rave workplace reviews to people they are desperate to push out and you've got a serial liar—"

"And someone to keep an eye on. Stalking can be very frightening, and it is a criminal offense in this state."

"Thank you for listening," said Diane, patting Lew's fore-arm. "I wouldn't feel right if I didn't share that information, even though I'm sure Judith Kerr hasn't done anything wrong around here. It's like the importance of being informed of where sexual predators are living. Know what I mean?"

# CHAPTER TWENTY-FOUR

**B**ack at his house after the morning meeting in Lew's office, Osborne was puttering about, getting himself a late lunch, when Mallory walked in the back door. "Hey, Dad, just stopped in to say good-bye. Josh and I are driving back to Chicago first thing in the morning. And thanks for everything, Dad. Josh has had a great time.

"He can't wait to come back and go muskie fishing with you. Any news on the murders of that couple from Evanston?" she asked, rattling on as she reached for a bag of wild rice from his cupboard, saying, "Hey, hope you don't mind if I take this? Can't find it in Chicago.

"So, Dad, back to the Powers story. I know people in my office will be asking me about it."

"No major breakthrough," said Osborne with a shake of his head as he spread peanut butter on a slice of whole wheat bread, "but Lew's got a few leads, including the news that Margo Powers was having an affair with some guy up here."

He knew better than to mention the sighting of Bill Kimble's car in the Powers driveway, as news travels fast in Loon Lake. Be wise to wait until after Lew had spoken with Bill. Instead he decided to ask about another person who'd been on his mind.

"You stayed in pretty good touch with Kara Kudelik, right?"

"Yes. And I feel bad I haven't seen her recently. Our lives changed so much after high school, but she was always a good friend. Terrible what happened. I don't suppose you know more about that, do you?"

"Lew is hoping to talk to friends of hers, see if they have any ideas or know of people she was seeing."

"She should definitely talk to Maddie Jensen. Maddie's been a close friend of hers since college and followed Kara up here to take a teaching job. She would certainly know what Kara's been up to since her divorce. Madison Jensen is her full name and I can probably find a phone number from one of my friends."

Osborne turned to his daughter. "Would you mind finding that number right now?" He set his sandwich aside. "Lew has been working round the clock. I insisted she take the afternoon off and get things done at home, so anything I can do to make her life easier . . ."

"I'm on the case, Dad," said Mallory with a grin. She pulled out one of the kitchen chairs and plopped herself down as she punched a number into her cell phone. "Hi, Lyn," she said to whoever answered, "you wouldn't happen to have a number for Maddie Jensen, would you? Great. Sure, I'll get off right now."

Mallory ended the call and looked at her dad. "Waiting. She's texting it to me. . . ." Her cell phone binged and Mallory looked down. "Great, got it." Osborne handed her a notepad and she wrote the number down. "Want me to try her? If she answers, I can at least arrange for the two of you to be in touch."

"Sure. And I'll talk to her if you reach her right now."

Mallory hit the number she had just received and waited. "Hi, Maddie, this is Mallory Osborne. Do you have a minute?" She gave a positive nod toward her father then explained why she was calling. She listened to a response and asked, "Mind if I put you on speaker, Maddie?"

Osborne sat down next to Mallory and said in a loud voice, "Hello, Maddie? I'm Dr. Paul Osborne, Mallory's father. I'm also the acting coroner for the town of Loon Lake and deputized to assist Chief Ferris and the Loon Lake Police investigating the murder of Kara Kudelik.

"I'm hoping you and I might talk sometime today or tomorrow? Mallory thought you might be able to help us learn some personal background—"

"Yes, of course, Dr. Osborne," said the woman, interrupting him, "whenever it's convenient for you is fine with me. When I heard about Kara, I was stunned. So, believe me, I would be happy to tell you anything that may help the police find who killed her—*anything.*"

Osborne gave Mallory a look of relief, then said, "In that case, I live out on Loon Lake Road about two miles off County C—"

"Oh, really? I'm on North Limberlost Road so you might be right around the corner from me. Do you want to meet now or later today?"

"Now would be great," said Osborne. "If you don't mind joining me and Mallory here at my place, I'll give you my address."

After writing down his address, Maddie said, "I should be there in a few minutes, Dr. Osborne."

Off her cell phone, Osborne turned to his daughter.

"Thank you, Mallory. She sounds pretty upset by the news of Kara's death and she'd love to tell us what she knows."

"Want me to stay, Dad?"

"That would be wise if you don't mind," said Osborne. "Maddie obviously knows you, and I'm sure she'll be more comfortable if you're here."

———

Standing at the kitchen window with Mallory beside him, Osborne watched Maddie Jensen climb out of a red Toyota SUV. He walked to the back door to hold it open before she could knock. "Please, come in, Maddie," he said. "I can't thank you enough for taking the time on a spur of the moment like this."

The woman, whose tight black curls were held back from her face in a ponytail, raised serious eyes to his. "I'm still devastated by the news. Please excuse me if I start crying again, okay? Kara was my best friend. . . ." Tears welled as she spoke.

Putting an arm around her shoulders, Osborne walked her into the kitchen, where Mallory was waiting at the kitchen table. She stood up as they walked in. "Hi, Maddie, Dad is so relieved that you've got the time to do this. Can I get you something to drink? Coffee? Water? Tea?"

"No, thank you," said Maddie, pulling out a chair and sitting down with a heavy sigh. "When I first heard the news that Kara was dead, I was sure she had committed suicide."

"W-h-a-a-t?" asked Osborne and Mallory in unison.

"Why would you think *that*?" asked Osborne.

"She was pretty crushed when this man she was in love with told her that if he got a divorce he would never marry again. Kara wanted nothing more than to be married and be a mom. I'm sure that's the only reason she took a chance on the guy. That's why she married that first goombah."

"Are you saying she was seeing a married man?" asked Mallory.

Maddie nodded. "And, you know, from the beginning I told her not to count on the creep. Well, I didn't call him a creep in front of Kara but I did tell her to give it up. 'That guy's been fooling around for years,' I said.

"But she wouldn't listen and I could see why."

Mallory opened her mouth to make a comment but Osborne signaled to her to remain quiet, to let Maddie keep talking.

"Kara's first husband had been such a loser. Couldn't hold a job, he drank, always at bars with the boys. Cute guy for what that's worth. So this time, she thought maybe she had found a man she could count on: charming, has money, told her he adored her. . . . The usual baloney."

"But he was married?" asked Osborne. "How did that make him someone she thought she could count on?"

"That's what I said." Maddie sat back in her chair. "And, *and* I even saw him out with another woman once. Not his wife. But I didn't tell Kara. Damn. I should have. I really should have." Her eyes misted with tears again.

"Who the hell is this guy?" asked Osborne.

Maddie turned away. "See, I knew you were going to ask

and . . . I can't say. I don't want to get anyone in trouble. I mean, I know he's not the one who did it."

Mallory leaned forward. "Maddie, your best friend has been murdered. You can't keep information like this confidential. Who knows? Maybe the man's wife . . ."

"Evie is not that kind of person," said Maddie. "She wouldn't know how—"

"Evie *Kimble?*" Osborne stood up. "Are you saying Bill Kimble is the man with whom Kara was involved?"

Maddie looked nervous. "Promise me you won't say who told you, Dr. Osborne? Bill Kimble is my cousin."

———————————

"I need to think about this before I approach Kimble," said Lew after Osborne reached her by phone where she was standing in her garden. "According to Bruce, we have a strong lead with the footprints found at the Powers place and Kara Kudelik's matching. We find the person who left those footprints and I've got something to go on.

"But nothing other than Margo and Kara's relationships with Bill Kimble point in his direction. A strange coincidence, I know, but not enough to say he's a person of interest . . . not yet anyway."

"Now wait," said Osborne. "Bill may know something else that links the two women," said Osborne. "You can accuse me of watching too much *Law & Order* but it could be as simple as some nutcase is out to teach him a lesson."

"Maybe a nutcase married to a different woman with whom Kimble has had an affair?" theorized Lew. "Not impossible, given that guy's bad behavior."

Lew was quiet for a moment before saying, "You're right, Doc. The fact he has been intimate with two women each of whom is now dead has to make you wonder. I'll give Kimble a call right now and tell him to meet me at the station first thing tomorrow morning. If he has a problem with that, I'll give up planting my tomatoes and go get the guy."

"Call me back after you talk to him, please? If you're going to meet with him now, someone needs to know."

Lew called back within five minutes. "It's okay, Doc, he sounded surprised. When he asked me what this is all about, I said that since Lillian's body was found on his property, I have questions I need to run by him.

"And, Doc, do you mind sitting in on that meeting?"

---

Off the phone, Osborne told Mallory the plan. Then he said, "There's something else I need to talk to you about, kiddo. Do you mind walking out onto the porch with me?"

"Oh, oh, Dad. What's up? You only ever want to talk to me on the porch when I've been bad." She chuckled as she spoke but her eyes were serious.

Sitting across from each other, Mallory on the wide porch swing and Osborne in his easy chair, he said, "This relationship you have with Josh worries me."

"Dad, please . . ."

"Hear me out, Mallory. He's almost twelve years younger than you. He's in his twenties and you're almost thirty-six years old. That's a big difference."

Mallory looked off toward the lake, thinking, then she smiled, stood up, and said, "How old are you, Dr. Osborne?"

"You know how old I am."

"How old is Lewellyn Ferris?"

"It's not the same."

"Answer me."

"She's . . . um . . . fifty-two."

"I rest my case."

"But—"

"And don't bring it up again." She leaned forward to give him a kiss on the cheek, squeezed his shoulder, and started to walk out of the room. She stopped at the doorway to the living room, turned, and said, "You're sweet to worry." And she was gone.

Osborne sat there feeling abashed. Well, that was a mistake, he thought to himself, what else can I do wrong?

His cell phone rang. "Doc?" asked Ray. "Just wanted to let you know that I'm planning to stake out that clearing again, next to where I found Lillian. See if the person who walked in there last night comes back. Whoever it was stepped right over the barriers the Wausau boys had set up to protect the crime scene. If they try it again, they'll meet a human owl . . . armed. Don't worry, I have a concealed-carry permit."

"Are you sure this is wise?" asked Osborne.

"That's why I'm telling you where I'll be."

# CHAPTER TWENTY-FIVE

Osborne was reading on his porch, all the windows open to the evening breezes and the melancholy echo of a loon calling, when the peace was broken by the trill of his cell phone.

"Lew? I thought you were planning an early night or I would have called," he said.

"You're right but just as I was drifting off I realized I'd forgotten to tell you that Diane Armeo caught up with me while I was gardening this afternoon. She wanted me to know that Ray's best friend, Judith, has been lying about her job history. The woman was never in the NSA. Diane said she checked with a former colleague to see what area she may have been working in but there is no record of a Judith Kerr ever being in the agency.

"Diane then ran a background check and learned Judith has quite a checkered employment history elsewhere. She has been fired numerous times, she's been accused of inappropriate behavior with male superiors, and she has falsified her résumé numerous times. Also, two police reports alleging she was stalking former boyfriends."

Lew took a breath. "Sorry, Doc, just wanted to be sure you knew all this before we see Kimble tomorrow."

"I can't say I'm surprised," said Osborne, leaning forward with his elbows on his knees, "growing up, some of the kids, especially Mallory, considered her a pathological liar. Did I tell you about the time she tried to get Mallory kicked out of an English class at a time when a good grade point was critical for her college applications?"

"You did. She accused Mallory of cheating on tests, right?"

"Judith went to the high school principal and said Mallory had been cheating on English exams. Mallory was beside herself and so worried. Her mother and I went up to meet with the principal and when he asked the English teacher about the cheating, the teacher was astounded that Judith had said that. 'Mallory couldn't cheat,' her teacher said. 'I give open-book tests. Judith is lying.'

"That was one episode of many in Judith's life in those days. She was a mixed-up kid then and, obviously, she's still pulling the same baloney. Good of Diane to alert you in case she pulls some funny stuff around here.

"Did I mention that Ray said she's been hanging all over Bill Kimble? At least she was when she hired Ray to guide them as a gift for Bill the other day. Apparently they renewed their friendship at their high school class reunion . . . if 'renew' and 'friendship' are the right words," he added.

"Can't say they might not deserve each other," said Lew. He could hear she was ready for sleep.

"One more thing," said Osborne. "Ray called me around seven to say he was planning to spend the night near the clearing where Lillian was found. Since that one intruder crossed the barriers protecting the crime scene last night, he's hoping they'll be back tonight."

"Some overdedicated birder no doubt. I do know he's there because Officer Adamczyk watched him park his truck a ways down the road and walk in near the crime scene. He called me to be sure it was okay for Ray to be there. I said it was and explained that we're hoping to find a birder who doesn't understand KEEP OUT signs or a Peeping Tom with no brains. You haven't heard more from Ray, have you?"

"No, and I'm sure I will if he sees anything or runs into trouble."

"No trouble, please," said Lew. "I need sleep."

She had just fallen asleep when her personal cell phone buzzed with a text message. It was from Bruce:

> Lab report just in. Bullet found in John Powers's skull is
> a match to the bullets dug out from the tree where Lillian
> Curran was killed. Same gun, Chief. More in the morning. B.

---

"We're looking for a twenty-two caliber pistol," said Bruce as Lew opened their early morning meeting. "The shooter used a subsonic round, which kept the sound of the gunshot down. That's why the neighbors on both sides of the Powers residence didn't hear anything that night.

"Those bullets may be quiet but they are dangerous. The one that killed John Powers penetrated the skull before spinning around inside the poor guy's head. One shot killed him. So"—Bruce laid both hands on the table—"that's what we're looking for: a twenty-two caliber pistol," he said in a matter-of-fact tone.

"You said you have a match to the bullets found in the trees where Lillian Curran was found, right?" asked Lew.

"Yes. Same gun, no question."

"What do you think, Doc?" Lew looked at Osborne.

"Ray called me early this morning, said there were no visitors to the clearing during the night. Could be they were scared off by the sight of Ray's pickup, though he did park it down the road a good hundred yards."

The phone on Lew's desk rang. She answered, said a few words, and hung up. "Bill Kimble is on his way down the hall. Bruce, I'd like you to sit in on this but don't say anything, please. Mr. Kimble is not expecting to be questioned about a few things and I have a plan."

"I understand," said Bruce, raising his eyebrows. He sat back in his chair, gave Osborne a quick glance, and pursed his lips.

A knock on her office door prompted Lew to walk over and let the visitor in. "Bill, you know Dr. Osborne," she said as she directed him to a chair in front of her desk, the one between Osborne and Bruce, "and I'd like you to meet Bruce Peters from the Wausau Crime Lab."

"Sure," said Bill, looking concerned, "is there some way I can help you folks?" He sat back in the chair and crossed his right leg over his left.

"Maybe, at least we hope so," said Lew with a gracious smile. "Bill, did you know Margo Powers?"

"Yes, I golfed with her husband, John. Very nice woman. I think everyone at the country club knew Margo and John.

Tragic what happened, but I understand it may be connected to John's business in some way."

"How *well* did you know Margo?" Lew asked, emphasizing the word *well*.

"Oh, you know, the usual."

"No, I don't know the usual. Incidentally, Bill, this is police business, so I am taping our conversation. Do you have a problem with that?"

"Not in the least, Chief Ferris. Like I said, I am here to help."

"About Margo Powers," said Lew. "Neighbors have reported seeing your car parked in the Powerses' driveway when John was out of town. Why were you there?"

Bill sat up and uncrossed his legs. "Um, I think that must have been the day she asked me to show her how to fly fish."

Osborne caught Lew's eye, signaling he was about to ask a question. After she nodded, he said, "You don't fly fish, Bill. Why would she ask you? And what could you show her?"

Bill squirmed and crossed his left leg over his right. "I should have said 'casting.' She wanted me to show her how to cast a fly rod." No one said anything. "I mean, you cast one rod you cast 'em all. Right?"

Lew jotted something down on a notepad in front of her. "And Kara Kudelik, Bill, did she need help with a fishing rod?"

Bill's face fell. He was silent.

"Bill, any other women you've been intimate with over the last six months?"

He worked his mouth before answering. "Patsy Carrington up in Eagle River. We play bridge in a group once a month."

"Bridge." Lew stated the one word and nothing more. She waited.

"What about Judith Kerr?" asked Osborne.

"Oh." Bill waved a dismissive hand. "That was once. Just once. I had too much to drink at my high school reunion."

"So just once doesn't count?" asked Lew.

"Well, maybe, I guess I've seen her four times. Twice before she came to visit."

"The question was how many women have you been intimate with over the last few months—not how many times. Now, Bill, of the women you've mentioned two have been murdered in the last week. Do you have any idea why? And by whom?"

Bill dropped his face into his hands. His shoulders shook, and Osborne wondered if he might hyperventilate. He watched the man's breathing, hoping they wouldn't have to call for medical help.

Finally Bill raised his head, took a deep breath, pushed his shoulders back, and turning to Osborne said, "Not me, I swear. Dr. Osborne, you know me, you knew my parents. You know I am not capable of doing such a terrible thing. Why would I?"

"Good question," said Lew. "That's what we're trying to figure out."

The room was quiet again. A semitrailer could be heard driving on the city street outside the courthouse. Bruce and Osborne sat without moving.

"Do I need to call a lawyer?"

"You may if you wish," said Lew. "I am not charging you with anything at this time."

Bill's face changed as he said, "What about Lillian Curran?

Someone shot that poor old lady and she is not someone I had anything to do with."

"In that case, Bill, do you have any idea why she was found dead just over the property line—*on your property?*" Again, Lew emphasized three words.

"We have reason to believe the gun that killed Margo and John Powers is the same gun used to kill Lillian Curran. Not positive yet but looking that way."

Bill was quiet, his eyes darting from Lew to Osborne to Bruce, as if they might be able to answer Lew's last question.

"What if I tell you that someone has been standing in the clearing near where Lillian's body was found and that individual may have been watching your house or your neighbors'—"

Before Lew could finish, Bill leaped to his feet: "It's me. I'm next, aren't I? Oh, my God, you've got to help me." He began to pace around the room. "They're after me. You have to stop—"

"Bill, sit down and be quiet, please," said Lew. "This may not be about you. Your wife could be the target. Have you had a relationship with your neighbor Erica Tolbert?"

"Good. God. No. I've only seen the woman once. It's her husband I have to deal with. So . . . you think they might be after Evie?" He relaxed slightly.

What a selfish bastard, thought Osborne, watching him. Okay if it's your wife, not you, huh. He glared at the man.

"Bill," said Lew, "I'll be talking to the sheriff's department today because I don't have the manpower to handle twenty-four-hour surveillance on your home and your neighbors' place. Until we know who has killed four people, each of whom had some connection to you, we will keep you and your family under surveillance. This is to protect you.

"Please tell your wife that each of you needs to let Dispatch here at the police station know when you have to leave, where you are going, and when you will be returning. Understand? I'll take care of informing the Tolberts, your next-door neighbors."

"Thank you. Thank you very much."

The man was so grateful, Osborne was convinced he was scared out of his mind. He did wonder how Bill was going to explain the situation to Evie. But then again—maybe she had always known.

―――――――――

After Bill left, Bruce excused himself, too. "We may have more ballistics data in on the gun or guns," he said. "I need to check with Ray to see what else he may have come across at the crime scene near the Kimbles' place."

After he walked out, Lew thought for a minute then said to Osborne, "You know, Doc, I can't talk to John and Margo Powers and I can't talk to Kara Kudelik but I sure as hell can ask Judith Kerr and Kimble's lady friend up in Eagle River, the one with whom he alleges he plays bridge, a few questions that are bugging me."

"Don't forget to ask Judith about her heroic days in the NSA," said Osborne, teasing.

"Right," said Lew with a smirk. "Give me a few minutes to touch base with the county sheriff's office and arrange for them to help with surveillance on the Kimble and Tolbert properties. Then let's head out to wherever it is that Judith

Kerr is staying. I'm hoping you don't mind sitting in on that conversation, too. I realize this is cutting into your time in the boat. . . ."

"Actually, it's the dog who misses me most. Poor Mike. Sure, let's do this. I've known Judith since she was a kid living next door, so she may be more comfortable with me there. Then again she may not," he said with a wry lift of his eyebrows.

"Do you know how to reach her? Or do you want me to check with Ray and see if he has a phone number and address?"

# CHAPTER TWENTY-SIX

The cottage that Judith Kerr had rented for the summer was one of the cabins belonging to the Three Brothers Resort. After driving past the main lodge, they could see the cottage set back from the road about a hundred yards. It had a shiny metal roof and appeared to be of recent construction. A black Jeep Wrangler was parked near the door to the cottage.

"I didn't get an answer when I tried the cell number Ray gave me," said Osborne. "Could be she's out for a walk or over on the tennis courts."

"Or a swim," said Lew. "Squirrel Lake is shallow, so the water here warms up early. If I were renting a cottage out here, I'd be down by the lake enjoying the sunshine."

Lew pulled her cruiser into a second parking space in front of the cottage. They got out of the car, walked up to the door, and, just as she was raising her hand to knock on the door, Lew glanced down. Hand in the air, she stared down. Osborne followed her gaze and saw what she saw: a pair of worn running shoes.

Leaning down, Lew picked up one shoe and turned it on its side. "New Balance," she said. She peered into the shoe.

"Size nine." She turned to Osborne and lowered her voice. "How many of these have you seen recently?"

Before he could answer, the cottage door swung open to reveal a tall, thin blond woman in tan cargo pants and a black T-shirt. Taken aback, she stared at the two of them before asking, "Dr. Osborne?" Her eyes shifted to Lew. "Who are you? What are you doing here?"

Ignoring the questions, Lew stepped forward. "Judith Kerr?"

"Y-e-s-s? Have we met?"

"I'm Lewellyn Ferris, chief of the Loon Lake Police, and I was at dinner last Friday night with Mallory and Dr. Osborne when you stopped by our table."

"Oh, I remember seeing Mallory. . . ."

"Dr. Osborne is Loon Lake's acting coroner and he is deputized to assist my department with homicide investigations," said Lew, her manner pleasant but brisk. "May we come in? We have a few questions regarding Loon Lake residents whom you may know."

"Really? I've been gone so long I really don't know many people anymore. I doubt I can help you. I'm just visiting, you know. But, all right, I guess you can come in."

Judith took a reluctant step back and out of their way. With Lew leading, they walked into a modest dining area, which anchored a spacious living room. Large plate glass windows filled the wall looking out over the lake.

"I grew up next door to the Osbornes. Did Dr. Osborne tell you?" she asked as the three of them sat down around a small kitchen table.

"He did," said Lew, pulling out a notepad. "Judith, how long have you known Bill Kimble?"

"So this is about Bill? Is he okay?"

"He's fine," said Lew, "and one of several people who grew up here that I want to ask you about."

"Oh, gosh, I hope my memory is good enough for you." Judith tipped her head back, thinking. "So how long have I known Bill, huh . . . since eighth grade maybe?" She smiled. "He took me to the Junior Prom our sophomore year . . . after Evie had turned him down."

"Was that the first time?" asked Lew.

"The first time for *what*?" asked Judith, a hint of irritation in her voice that disappeared by the time she said, "The first date? Yes, why."

"Just trying to connect the dots," said Lew. "How well did you know Kara Kudelik?"

"I don't know any Kudelik," said Judith. "Oh, wait, did I see a death notice for her in the crummy Daily Snooze that passes for a newspaper around here? Oh wait . . . the more I think about it . . . maybe she was in my class. But I never really knew her. She was a swimmer. I hated sports. Yeah, now I remember a Kudelik, but I would never recognize her today."

"Like you, she was a good friend of Bill Kimble's, so I assumed you might know her, too," said Lew matter-of-factly. "And how about Margo Powers? Was she in the same class as you and Bill?"

"Never heard of the woman." Judith's eyes searched Osborne's, a crafty expression flashing across her face. He had a sudden memory of a little girl deliberately smashing the

Halloween pumpkin that Mallory had labored over and, later, denying she had done it even though Osborne, watching from their living room window, had seen her do it. Denied it with the same exact expression he had just seen cross her features.

"You're sure?" asked Lew. "The name Margo Powers doesn't ring a bell?"

With a shrug of impatience implying she had answered enough questions, Judith reached for an iPhone, which was sitting on the counter behind her, and started to scroll for messages. She ignored the question.

"How about Patsy Carrington?" Lew made a show of checking a list on her notepad as if this was one more name among others.

"Who?" Judith sounded preoccupied.

"Bill Kimble's good friend from Eagle River."

Dropping the phone onto the table, Judith looked up with a face of thunder. *"Who?"*

"Never mind," said Lew. "I can see you don't know her."

"I don't. Who else don't I know?"

"Lillian Curran?"

"That nosy old lady? Of course I know her. When I was a kid, she lived up on the hill in a big white house. Knew who she was is all."

"How do you know she was nosy?" asked Lew.

"Um . . . ," Judith stammered. "Bill. Bill told me she was always hanging around their property. He didn't know why and it bothered him."

"She loved to bird-watch," said Osborne. "For the last few weeks she's been watching a great horned owl that has a nest not far from the Kimbles' house. She was very protective of that owl, which irritated some of the other birders. Maybe they said she was 'nosy'?" He did his best to sound friendly, as he could sense Lew closing in.

"And she's dead," said Lew. "Someone shot and killed her while she was watching that magnificent bird."

"I heard," said Judith, "too bad, but serves her right for trespassing in the middle of the night."

"How do you know she was shot in the middle of the night?" asked Lew. "We haven't released the circumstances of how Lillian died to the press."

"Bill told me," said Judith with an airy wave of her hand as she stood up. "People, I have a hair appointment in a few minutes and need to leave. You can call me if you have more questions."

"Before you go, I want to know *specifically* how you know the circumstances of Lillian's death," said Lew, getting to her feet, "because Bill Kimble has been under strict orders not to discuss that with anyone other than law enforcement."

Judith walked over to one corner of the tiny kitchen area and reached for a red leather purse sitting on the counter. Slinging the purse across her body, she unzipped the purse, reached in, and pulled out a small handgun. Pointing it at Osborne and Lew, she said, "Chief Ferris, take off your belt and lay it carefully on the table. Dr. Osborne, empty your pockets. Then both of you keep your hands high where I can see them."

Lew did as she was told, which meant both of her cell phones, her pager, her holster with her trusty Sig Sauer .40 caliber semiautomatic, and the keys for the cruiser were all on the small kitchen table. Osborne added his wallet, cell phone, two quarters, and the keys to his car.

"Chief Ferris, you're lucky," said Judith, her gun pointing at the two of them. "Years ago, many years ago, Dr. Osborne was the one person who always smiled at me. One day I fell off my bicycle and he took the time to put three Band-Aids on my knee so I wouldn't bleed all over my pants and make my mom hit me.

"That means I don't want to shoot him. You? I don't care but what the hell. I'll be long gone before you can do anything. See that closet by the door?" She waved her gun. "I want you both in there . . . now. Right now."

As they walked toward the closet, Lew asked, "Is it Evie you want?"

"No. I want what she *has*. I always have."

The closet had no clothes hanging, so Osborne was able to push the few hangers to one side, but the ceiling was so low that in order to squeeze in he had to get down on his knees. Without saying a word, Lew pushed her way in beside him.

The door closed and a lock turned. The closet was so stuffy Osborne had to tilt his head back and over Lew's in order to get as much air as possible. He was sure Lew had to be even more uncomfortable. He heard rustling sounds from inside the cottage, then a door slammed shut. A minute or two passed, both of them holding their breath so as not to make a noise. Then the sound of a car driving away.

Another few minutes passed and no sound of anyone entering the cottage. Lew whispered, "Let's give it another five minutes, Doc. Just in case . . ."

They had to be the longest five minutes Osborne had

lived in years. At last Lew's shoulders shifted and she whispered, "Okay. Should be safe. The door has a child lock. Thank God for new cabins." Lew pressed a toggle on the door, a loud click, and the knob turned. Still, they waited, listening.

# CHAPTER TWENTY-SEVEN

L ew crept out of the closet, paused, listened, then opened the door wide for Osborne to fall forward into the room. A quick glance at the table in the dining area showed Lew's belt and his wallet and keys were gone.

"Hurry, Doc," said Lew, waiting as he shook out his cramped legs. She opened the front door. Only her cruiser was parked outside. The Jeep was gone.

"Main lodge is our best bet," cried Lew as she dashed out of the cottage, Osborne following.

They ran across the road and over an asphalt playground to the back entrance for the lodge. Then down a long, dark hallway past an empty swimming pool to the main desk, where a woman was sitting. Ignoring the woman's startled expression as they ran at her, Lew held out her badge, talking fast as she reached for the guest phone sitting on the counter.

She hit o for an outside line and reached Dispatch. After explaining what had happened, Lew said, "I need a squad car out here at Three Brothers ASAP. Alert the Kimbles, the Tolberts, and Officer Adamczyk to watch for the subject in case she has decided to approach the Kimble property. Then call a woman in Eagle River by the name of Patsy Carrington and alert her, too. I have no idea what Judith Kerr is planning to do next. Tell everyone she's armed and dangerous—got it?"

By the time she had finished speaking, a siren could be heard in the distance. Lew threw the phone down. "I'm going back to the cottage, Doc, on the off chance that that woman left my phones behind. If she's got any tech smarts, she'll know she can be traced by the signals from my cell phones. Pick me up there."

Lew took off down the dark hallway and Osborne ran out to the front of the main lodge just as Officer Donovan pulled up. "That way, Todd," said Osborne, pointing down the road and around a corner leading to the cottage.

As they drove up, Lew was standing in front of her cruiser waving her arms. Osborne was surprised to see she had buckled on her belt. She ran over to the driver's side of the squad car, shouting, "It's okay. I got everything, even my gun. She threw my belt into the shrubbery over there. Please, you two, remind me to never, ever wear all critical gear in one place ever again. Stupid. Goddamn stupid."

She hurried over to where Osborne was climbing out of the squad car. "Doc, here's your wallet and keys. Hurry up and get in my cruiser. Officer Donovan, follow me. I'll be checking with Dispatch to see if Officer Adamczyk—"

Both her cell phones rang simultaneously. Lew answered one, saying, "It's okay. It's me. I found my phones . . . what?" She listened then clicked off.

"A 911 call just came in from one of the Kimble numbers but it went dead." She spun the cruiser around to head back down the resort lane to the main road. "Hold on, Doc, this may not be fun."

Bent over the steering wheel, eyes focused on the road as she sped over the rises and around corners, Lew had a look on her face that reminded Osborne of the mother bear who had chased himself and Ray when they were mushroom hunting and stumbled onto an ancient uprooted hemlock serving as a den sheltering two young cubs. That bear's rush in their direction was not a warning: she was out to kill. That was the day Osborne was thankful the locks on Ray's beat-up pickup didn't work.

Keeping both hands on the steering wheel as she sped down the road, Lew called in to Dispatch through the cruiser's Bluetooth. As she listened, Osborne saw her face tighten. "No word from Officer Adamczyk, either? Not answering his cell? That's not good. Call the sheriff's department again. Yes, I know you told them I need backup, but tell them we have a man down. Then call the EMTs. Be sure they know we have a shooter."

The squad car assigned to Roger Adamczyk was parked on the county road between the driveways leading to the Kimble and Tolbert homes. From that vantage point, he would have been able to see any vehicles entering and leaving those properties. Straight ahead of where he was parked, yellow tape was in place marking the perimeters of the crime scene where Lillian Curran's body had been found.

As Lew drew closer to the squad car, Osborne could see one of the rear windows was shattered.

"Oh, no," said Lew under her breath. "Roger has always worried he might get caught in a bad situation. Poor guy."

She pulled up behind the squad car and, leaving the

cruiser running, opened her door, slipped out, and crouched low. "Stay here, Doc, and keep your head down. Let me check first." She crept forward to the driver's door of the squad car.

Without standing up, she reached for the door handle, paused to listen, and when there was no sound, pulled the door open a crack. "Roger?" she whispered. "Are you in here?"

A muffled "Yes" came back. "I'm on the floor, Chief."

Now Lew could make out a pant leg through the crack in the door. "Are you hit?"

"No. But I ain't movin'. That woman's got a gun."

"You saw her? Before I got here?"

"Yeah, maybe ten minutes ago. Dispatch told me to watch for a black Jeep and right then she drove at me. Guess she saw me sitting here. Shot out the window, but I'm okay."

"Do you know which driveway she drove down?"

"Kimble. I heard more shots, too. Just a minute or so ago. Be careful, Chief."

As she was whispering, Lew could hear the crunching of cars driving the gravel road and pulling in behind her. She was relieved that the sheriff and his deputies had driven in without their sirens wailing.

"Stay here, Roger, until I tell you to come out."

She crept back to the cruiser. Once inside, she motioned to Osborne to stay crouched in his seat while she reached Dispatch. "Put me through to the sheriff or one of his people who are out here, please? Not sure if it's safe to get out of the car."

Connected immediately, she told the officer on the phone that Judith Kerr was believed to be near or in the Kimble home. "I have no idea what she is likely to do," said Lew. "My plan is to get Bill and Evie Kimble out of there alive without any of us getting hit."

She listened. "Yes, the woman is armed. I don't know the scope of her problems or her intentions but I'm hoping we can negotiate with her. That would be our best outcome . . . the road is blocked? Good."

While she listened for another few seconds, Osborne raised his head to peer out the window. The midafternoon sun was shining, the leaves on the birch trees lining the road a rich green. He inched the window down and got a breath of fresh air. The world was silent. All seemed good except . . .

"Doc, wait here. You're not armed or trained for this. I'm starting in and Sheriff Richards will be with me."

"Be very careful, Lewellyn," said Osborne. "I have fresh walleye fillets for dinner." He felt like bawling as he spoke.

Lew reached over to squeeze his arm. "I have grandchildren, too," she said and slipped out the door.

———

Lew started down the driveway toward the large house. Sheriff Richards, whom she met with weekly to review county issues, had gotten out of his vehicle and, gun drawn, followed behind her by ten feet. They made eye contact, said nothing, and moved slowly forward.

Lew made a decision to avoid the driveway, moving instead through the trees lining the paved drive, which would give them some cover. They had a view of the front and one side of the Kimble home. The side of the house that was visible appeared to have a porch opening onto a deck. Beyond the deck, Lew could see a short path leading to the lake. At the end of the path was a long dock with a canopy boat lift set alongside.

A door slammed and Lew jumped, startled. She stopped, looked back at Sheriff Richards, and saw that he had heard the noise, too. They stood still, both of them, waiting and watching. The deck was empty though Lew was pretty sure it was a door to the porch that they had heard.

A door slammed again and now Lew saw Judith standing on the deck with Bill Kimble walking ahead of her. The two stopped. Lew saw Judith prod Bill with her gun, and he moved forward.

The sound of a gunshot caused Judith and Bill to duck and start running down the path to the dock. Judith stumbled, and her gun flew out of her hand. Seeing she was unarmed, Lew was about to run after Judith when she saw the woman bend to reach into a low front pocket of her cargo pants and pull out another handgun. She turned, aiming in Lew's direction. Another shot rang out. Judith shoved her gun into Bill's back, forcing him onto the dock.

Unsure where the gunfire was coming from, Lew turned to see it was Sheriff Richards firing. "Warning shots," he shouted. "Get down, Chief."

Later he would admit that firing the warnings might not have been the smartest move. "I thought I could scare the shit out of that woman," he would say.

"Well, you scared them, all right," said Lew. But that was later.

Forced to run ahead of Judith, Bill scrambled into the speedboat moored under the canopy. Judith climbed in behind him. The lift motor went on, dropping the boat into the water. The sound of the inboard starting up could be heard and Lew could see Judith in the captain's chair, driving.

Lew raised her gun, prepared to fire into the boat, hoping to damage the motor. As she leveled her gun in the direction of the speedboat, a pontoon filled with people came into view. If I miss, thought Lew, I could hit someone on that pontoon. She lowered her gun.

As the boat pulled away, both she and Sheriff Richards were on their cell phones, alerting law enforcement up and down the chain of lakes where boat landings could give Judith an opportunity to hide before forcing Bill Kimble to drive north with her. If she could get that far, an escape to Canada was only an hour away.

"With that pontoon behind them, I didn't dare fire," said Lew, running toward the house. "Sheriff Richards, I'm very worried about—"

Before Lew could say more a woman ran out of the front door of the house: Evie Kimble.

"Evie, are you all right?" asked Lew, rushing toward her.

"I think so," said the petite, dark-haired woman. "Bill was in the kitchen when she came in. I could hear them talking. He was furious but she was . . . I was so scared. I locked myself in the bedroom and hid under the bed."

Evie peered beyond Lew and the sheriff. "Where is Bill? Did she hurt him? She was so angry. I don't understand."

While she was talking Lew turned to follow Sheriff Richards down to the dock. Hurrying out to the far end of the dock, he said, "I want to know which way they go at that fork by the island. Do they take the channel?"

As the three of them stood on the dock watching the boat

in the distance, they saw it turn toward the channel, still traveling at a high speed. In less than ten seconds the boat was airborne forty feet or more. It seemed to hover overhead before it landed and burst into flames.

"Did I really see that?" Lew was too stunned to believe what she was seeing. "Oh no," she said under her breath. "Those damn kids moved the channel markers again."

# CHAPTER TWENTY-EIGHT

Lew's office was quiet as four people seated around the small coffee table under the big windows sat waiting. It was a Friday morning in late June and court had adjourned early for the weekend, so the sidewalks and lawn were empty.

"She should be here any minute," said Lew, breaking the silence. "Evie spent the night at her parents' home in Rhinelander. I offered to put this meeting off until Monday but she insisted she wants to get it over."

"Here she comes," said Ray who had spotted a lone figure walking up toward the main entrance to the courthouse. As they all turned to watch, Evie Kimble walked along in front of the windows and down the side walkway toward the entrance to the Loon Lake Police Department.

"Good morning, Chief Ferris," she said moments later as she walked through the door.

"Let me introduce you to Bruce Peters with the Wausau Crime Lab," said Lew, guiding Evie toward a chair at one end of the coffee table. "He needs to be here and he may have questions for you . . . if you're up to it. I don't think any of us can fully understand the impact of what you've been through over the last twenty-four hours."

Evie managed a slight smile. Osborne found it interesting that she didn't appear to have circles or redness around her eyes. Was her overwhelming emotion relief?

"I was hiding during the scariest time," said Evie. "Under my bed," she added with a glance at Bruce in case he hadn't heard earlier.

"Had you met Judith Kerr before yesterday?" asked Bruce. "And, please, stop if there is anything you feel you can't discuss yet."

"I think I'll be fine," said Evie. "Yes, and Dr. Osborne knows this," she said, looking over at Osborne as she spoke. "We grew up going to the same junior high and high school. I really never saw her after graduation, though, until our high school reunion in May.

"I saw her then when she came up to talk with me and Bill but not since, until yesterday."

"Can you tell us exactly what you saw yesterday?"

"Certainly. I was in my downstairs sewing room working on a quilt when I heard a car drive up. I looked out the basement window and saw Judith walking toward the house. Not sure what happened next because I didn't hear the doorbell ring. I guess she must have just walked in without knocking or anything.

"Next thing I heard was Bill shouting and that's when I got scared. Bill and I have separate bedrooms and mine is at the bottom of the stairs next to my sewing room. First I locked myself in there and decided to wait until they stopped fighting. Then I heard a gunshot. That's when I hid under the bed."

"She fired at the coffeemaker sitting on the counter," said Bruce. "We assume it was to scare your husband."

"I guess she did because he left with her, didn't he," said Evie. "That's all I can tell you. I stayed under the bed until things seemed quiet. I guess you know I called 911 and that's when they told me to stay in the house and all the police were there. I didn't dare go outside until I saw the boat leave and Sheriff Richards out in the yard with his gun.

"What I don't understand and maybe you can tell me is why our boat exploded. Bill loved to water-ski and he kept that speedboat in excellent condition."

"Nothing was wrong with the boat," said Lew. "We've had a rash of kids, local teenagers, who've thought it was funny to keep moving the buoy markers in the channel. You know, the ones that alert people to the huge boulders scattered through there and difficult to see because of Loon Lake's dark water."

"I know that, but everyone knows to go slow," said Evie.

"You're right," said Lew. "Even tourists who haven't been on the lake before know enough to follow the NO WAKE signs. We know Judith was driving the boat and had that throttle wide open yesterday—"

"I'm sure it's been years since she's driven through the Loon Lake channels," said Osborne. "Add to that the drought we've been experiencing in the northwoods, so water levels have been low. She didn't realize what she was heading into."

"Would it have made a difference?" asked Lew dryly. "We were bound to catch up with her eventually. Knowing what we know now about her intent to kill the women she considered her rivals, I think she would have tried to hold law enforcement off at gunpoint and we can only imagine how that might have ended."

"Chief Ferris, you told me yesterday that she shot both

the Powerses. I didn't know them. And she killed Kara, too?" asked Evie. "Guess I wasn't listening when you told me." She shrugged apologetically. "I had a lot to take in yesterday, sorry."

"Not with a gun," said Bruce, sitting forward, his eyebrows in a frown. "Kara Kudelik was hit hard in the back of her head, multiple times, with a heavy cast-iron skillet. My guess is she never knew what hit her. It looked to us like she had welcomed that woman into her home. There were two full cups of coffee and a plate of cookies on a little table in the living room." He raised his eyebrows as he said, "All untouched. Pretty sad.

"I am pleased to say, however, that a search of Kara's yard turned up a set of footprints that matched footprints we found at the home of John and Margo Powers, so we have tied Judith to that crime, too. But there's more, Evie, and you may find this disturbing, I'm afraid.

"Ray Pradt found a set of identical footprints near the spot where Lillian Curran's body was found." He waited before adding, "Judith had been out there watching your house."

Evie shuddered. "You're sure? That is so creepy. You know I'm going to sell that house. I sure don't want my real estate agent to hear that. You have other proof that Judith was the person behind all this, don't you?"

"Yes, indeed," said Bruce, "my forensic team has done a terrific job on the ballistics. We can prove the bullets that killed the Powers couple came from the same gun used on Lillian Curran who, you know, we found dead on your property.

"When she was running for the boat and forcing your husband to go along, she tripped and dropped the gun she had in her hand. That gun is the same one she used to shoot Lillian and the Powerses, too. Now she had another gun on her, and a check of the gun registry shows she owned numerous guns. We found two in her car and authorities in Minnesota are searching her condo over in the cities. I'm sure they'll find more there.

"One final confirmation that Judith has been behind all these murders is a used Kleenex that Ray found in his search of the clearing on your land. The DNA on that is a match to Judith Kerr, too."

"One thing I don't understand," said Evie, "is why on earth she killed that poor old woman? She had nothing to do with Bill."

"That's what we want to ask you," said Lew. "Do you have any idea why?"

Evie sat with a perplexed look on her face. "Well, there's only one thing I can think of and I doubt it has anything to do with this. . . ."

"Give us a try," said Bruce, hitching his chair closer to the coffee table.

"Lillian knocked on my door a couple months ago and asked permission to walk in the woods along the south side of our driveway. She said she thought an owl might be nesting somewhere in there and that she wanted to look for it after dark.

"I told her to go right ahead. I do some bird-watching my-self. A couple times late at night—and this has been in the last two weeks, by the way—I saw a light out there from my sew-ing room window, which is right under the kitchen. I assumed it was Lillian."

"Did Bill know about this?"

"No," said Evie, regret in her voice. "These last few years Bill and I didn't talk that much. I didn't say anything about the light because if I mentioned Lillian and birds I knew he'd think I was being silly."

"Lillian would not have been shining a light you could see from the house," said Ray, who had been quiet during the discussion. "That would have alerted the great horned owl she was trying to watch.

"It had to be Judith Kerr. I think Lillian saw her out there and told her she was trespassing and, knowing Lillian, I bet she got nasty and told Judith that if she ran into her again, she'd call the cops. We know now that Judith was not about to let that happen."

"Ray's right," said Lew.

"I have a question, Evie," said Osborne. "But it's a difficult one and I hope you don't mind. Did you know Bill was seeing Margo Powers? Or Kara?"

"Or any number of other women over the twelve years we've been married?" asked Evie with a grim hint of humor.

"Yes and no. Bill's playing around became clear to me about . . . oh . . . six weeks after our wedding. Do you believe he slept with one of my good friends the night before we were married? So I didn't know about those two women, but there have been so many over the years. At first I confronted him, I told him how hurtful it was, how he was not treating me as a friend, much less a wife—and he would promise to be faithful.

"Then it would happen again—and again." She gave a little laugh. "I didn't know there were that many women around here to sleep with.

"At first I couldn't understand it. I mean—why? I know I'm not that unattractive. He's the one who insisted on getting married. So why?

"I don't know." Evie shook her head. "I'm sure I could have gone to a therapist, but I didn't. I decided after the tenth time that there were enough good things about our marriage: I had a nice house, I didn't have to work, I could do my quilting and travel with my girlfriends. . . . It was more convenient to stay married than start over.

"Frankly, every year it got more convenient. Plus"—she gave a sheepish look—"I didn't have to sleep with him. Not very often anyway.

"Do I sound horrible?" She looked like she was going to cry.

"No," said Lew, reaching over to pat her hand, "pragmatic. You sound pragmatic."

"Evie," said Bruce, "as you know, we recovered the bodies late last night and your husband's is at our morgue in Wausau. Given the nature of his death an autopsy is required, but I don't think that will show any more than what we know already, which is that he died in the explosion. I expect his body to be released later today."

"Thank you," said Evie. "I'll make arrangements after I leave here. My parents will help me."

After Evie left, Bruce got to his feet, saying, "Well, Chief Ferris, I was gonna try and snag you for one more afternoon on the Prairie River but I'm afraid I just want to go home and snuggle with my wife."

# CHAPTER TWENTY-NINE

That evening as the sun was sprinkling diamonds across Loon Lake, Osborne and Lew sat relaxing in the Adirondack chairs he liked to keep on his dock for nights like this. At the sound of footsteps along the path leading from Ray's place, Osborne opened the can of ginger ale he had brought down, expecting a visitor.

"Anybody home?" asked Ray as he walked onto the dock, picked up his soda, and took over the weathered pine rocking chair next to Osborne. As if to welcome the newcomer, two fish leaped from the water.

"Oh, golly," said Ray, "there go two unlucky Ephemeroptera."

"Who?" asked Osborne.

"That's Latin for 'mayfly,'" said Ray, "I'm an educated man, doncha know."

His demeanor changed. "Not to ruin your evening, folks, but I've been puzzling over how someone becomes as disturbed as Judith Kerr. She was older than me growing up but I knew who she was. Remember, Doc, when I was a kid my parents lived just two blocks away from your house on Elm

Court and Judith and her mother lived on that block, too. She never struck me as someone who would grow up and—"

"—Become a psychopath?" Lew finished his question for him.

"You knew Judith as a child, Doc," said Lew. "What's your take on the woman? Where do you think behavior like hers comes from?"

"All I know is that as a little kid, she had a very hard life," said Osborne. "Her father walked out on Judith and her mother when she was four years old. And her mother was never a happy, even considerate, person. Summer nights when we had our windows open, we could hear her screaming at little Judith.

"Then there were days when I was home from the office for lunch, I would see Judith playing in our sandbox and she looked like no one took care of her. Her hair wasn't brushed, her clothes dirty. I fault that mother of hers. The woman was just plain mean.

"Just to give you an idea, after she was divorced from Judith's father, she married again, and that poor guy, two years into their marriage, committed suicide. So who knows? We never know what goes on behind closed doors.

"I think Judith grew up so desperate for love she grabbed whatever resembled it until that need became an obsession."

"I do have one good memory of her from when we were kids," said Ray. "She had this little bird, a wren, I think, that she had found. It had a broken wing and she was nursing it back to health. I remember her going around with that little bird sitting on her shoulder, tucked under the collar of her shirt.

"Then the bird got better and flew away. But one day

when a bunch of us kids were playing in your yard, Doc, and Judith was there, too, a bird flew out of nowhere and landed on her shoulder. It was amazing. Then it flew off, but she was so happy. She was sure it was *her* bird."

Ray was quiet for a moment before he said, "That might have been the only time I ever saw her genuinely happy."

"Too bad she didn't have the same empathy for human beings," said Lew. "It's funny but I've learned from my own life and from my experiences as a police officer that people who have a difficult start in life go one of two ways: either they survive and become productive human beings or they go bad and end up in prison or worse. We all make a choice."

Two hours later, in his bedroom with the windows wide open, Osborne lay listening to the hooting of owls, maybe the great horned owl, lonely in the night. He rested a light hand on the arm of the woman sleeping beside him: happy to have the friendship of a wise, kind woman; happy not to be alone.

# ACKNOWLEDGMENTS

A warm thank-you to everyone who has worked to make me look good: my editor, Jackie Cantor; her assistant, Sara Quaranta; our copyeditor, Shelly Perron; all the production team; and, especially, the designer of my lovely book jacket, Emma Van Deun. A special thank-you to my wonderful, supportive agent, Nell Pierce.